The Golden Cockatrice

When Paul Harris's Singapore-based shipping line is regularly undercut by a rival operating from Macao, Harris flies to Macao to investigate. And almost at once an old enemy crosses his path. Then an unexpected – and involuntary – visit to a tycoon's yacht and a tempting business offer leave Harris impressed but suspicious. Warily he decides to play for time.

But much to his chagrin, his stay in Macao is prolonged – again involuntarily – and by the same forces who arranged his visit to the yacht. The one bonus is his meeting with Wei, the attractive Chinese girl, who gives him the low-down on the tycoon. He also encounters two odd Americans, who say they are working among refugees.

A series of disturbing incidents leads Harris to realize that he is nothing but a pawn in an international power game, but it is one in which his allies and enemies prove unexpected, and his own life is dramatically at stake.

by the same author

The Golden Cockatrice

Gavin Black

The Crime Club
Collins, 14 St James's Place, London

William Collins Sons & Co Ltd
London . Glasgow . Sydney · Auckland
Toronto · Johannesburg

First published 1974
© Gavin Black, 1974
ISBN 0 00 231259 X
Set in Intertype Baskerville
Made and Printed in Great Britain by
William Collins Sons & Co Ltd Glasgow

'Cockatrice . . . a fabulous monster produced from a cock's egg hatched by a serpent, it was believed to possess the most deadly powers, plants withering at its touch and men and animals dying poisoned by its look.'

Encyclopaedia Britannica.

CHAPTER 1

No one had told me that the old ferry boat between Hong Kong and Macao was offering mid-afternoon strip-tease in a desperate bid to compete with the much quicker hydrofoil service, and when the smoking-room was suddenly darkened I hadn't a clue what was coming. However, people round about seemed to be taking the sudden happening calmly enough, so I sat on in my chair savouring the unique travel experience of drinking iced beer in a blackout. Then two spotlights came on, one red, the other green, both shining towards the door to the steward's pantry. This was screened by a curtain swaying to the gentle rolling.

I must have been still fuzzed by the flight from Singapore for it wasn't until there was a scraping of chairs being re-positioned that I realized we were in for free entertainment. Canned music confirmed this, Eastern-bazaar type from an old Hollywood sound-track. Then the curtain was zipped back to reveal a woman wearing the costume which has more or less remained standard for a couple of thousand years since Salome first started this act, yards of some semi-transparent material wrapped around a body whose brightly painted nipples were already showing through it. She didn't gyrate at all, just stood there giving us our first long look, which was longer than I wanted.

The lady certainly took her time about getting into the beat of the music, her stomach coming into action first in an anti-clockwise movement that was very slow indeed, as though her physiotherapist had warned her that she had been overdoing recently. Then one arm came up, followed by the other, and she advanced towards us,

abdomen first. It was all of two minutes before the first veil
dropped. I couldn't really see how many more there were
to fall, but tradition made these at least six before that
final revelation of a mound of Venus, and as yet the
audience didn't seem at all impatient, no clapping had
started.

Around the table next to mine sat five Japanese business
men obviously taking time off from one of their intensive
drives to undermine the British commercial position in
Hong Kong. Like most of their countrymen out in the
world they were assuming that no one round about could
possibly understand their language, which I do in a patchy
sort of way, enough certainly to appreciate just how un-
complimentary their comment was. They were making it
quite plain that if this poor woman's weaving about was a
foretaste of what was available in the Far East's Tangier
then the shine was already off their prospects for a really
relaxing stay.

I waited for the third veil to drop before getting up and
making my way out on deck, which was rude to an artiste,
but I couldn't help it, I needed air. The view from the
rail was of lumpy little Chinese islands set down like
individual steamed puddings in the browny-blue sauce of
a Chinese sea. The usual square-sailed junks were pictur-
esque enough, though likely to be engaged in heroin smuggling as a sideline to fishing. There was a grey corvette
to aft of us, almost certainly British, showing the flag in
the only colonial waters left in which they can do this
and doubling that duty with the less pleasant one of trying
to intercept more refugees from the mainland travelling in
a desperate bid to switch allegiance from Mao to Queen
Elizabeth II.

'So you don't care for striptease either?' a voice said
behind me. 'I was born too long ago to be eligible for the
permissive society. But that doesn't apply to you.'

I turned and said: 'Doesn't it?'

A little woman, well under average height, but still angular and sharp-edged, not dumpy at all, was standing looking up at me. She was smiling. She had the kind of bridgework in which the auxiliary teeth are supported right on your own gums. It costs a lot to do and she appeared to have every confidence in it.

'I followed you out,' she said. 'It seemed a good lead.'

Sometimes looking at it in a mirror I wonder if I have a kind face. I can't see it, but people with a long history of getting the sharp brush-off from most of the world seem to zero in on me.

'On holiday in the Orient?' I asked politely.

'Well, not really. I've been doing a year's exchange teaching in Hong Kong.'

'Where were you exchanged from?'

'Boonville, Missouri.'

These academic walkabouts fascinate me. Nowadays a schoolteacher can get anywhere and find a salary waiting.

'Does that mean a Hong Kong Chinese has gone to Missouri?'

'That's right.'

'How's she liking Boonville?'

'Loves it.'

'How do you like Hong Kong?'

'Hate it.'

I don't usually find something in common with new contacts quite so quickly. The rail she was leaning against was almost level with what seemed to be buttoned-down breasts under a tight mauve-grey two-piece seersucker.

'I'm Amelia Jackson. What's your name?'

'Paul Harris.'

'That's Scotch, isn't it?'

'Yes.'

'My grandfather was Scotch. He came out to Missouri from somewhere near Aberdeen, Scotland, in 1886. A farmer. Would you believe it, three times his barns were taken by tornadoes. Carried clean over into the next county. But he just built another. He died worth a quarter of a million dollars.'

'Nice for the family.'

She shook her head.

'The money didn't come down my side at all. I've always thought myself really poor and fixed to stay that way . . . until I came out here.'

'And now?'

'Now I see that poverty is relative. What I thought it was has nothing to do with the real thing. You get the real thing in these parts. Death walking as a near skeleton in the streets while a Rolls-Royce passes.'

It was as good a description of Hong Kong as I've heard, earning her the drink I offered.

'I've never taken to alcohol, young man,' she said, flattering me. 'But I'll have a Coca-Cola with you.'

We went along to the deck bar and Miss Jackson sat perched up on the stool I had helped her to mount, sipping at that beverage which is one of the most conspicuous symbols of the West's deep penetration of Oriental patterns. Miss Jackson had a small apartment in Hong Kong which was a third of the way up the Peak and her block had just escaped the spring floods after a typhoon which had undermined another building exactly like hers, collapsing it with a death roll of seventeen people. She preferred tornadoes to typhoons.

'Have you ever been to Missouri, Mr Harris?'

'I've flown over it.'

'That's what most people do. You on holiday, too?'

'Not exactly. I have a business problem to sort out and it seemed a good idea to get away to some place I didn't know to do a little brooding.'

This was skirting the truth. I was travelling to the Portuguese colony to do some detective work of the kind that a good deal of contemporary business renders essential these days. Mrs Nivalahannanda, my co-director and our company trouble-shooter, had wanted the job but, although she has flair and an often highly successful intuitive approach, I didn't think the situation called for either of these talents, just some quiet snooping. Ranya would be no good at that, she can't fade into backgrounds, inevitably memorable in all her appearances.

We also have a personal problem I have been trying to get into perspective for some time now and thought I might do this by being a long way from the office. As a practical Thai girl Ranya thinks the logical thing to do is marry the boss. As she sees it I need plenty of the kind of sex she is ready and willing to give, and she may well be right, but I'm a romantic who can't warm to the idea of setting up house with a woman who, immediately after coitus, sits up in bed to tell me that we are moving far too many of our ships underloaded and that we must reassess our port network. This is vital stuff over morning coffee but it is not what a man wants to be served at midnight. Ranya just can't seem to understand. She keeps telling me that she is skilled in sex, even the husband she divorced had no complaints on this score, and she won't see that he may have been driven to his call girls by talk about their Thailand bus company schedules when it should have been how marvellous he was. She can be so beautiful it stops the heart and then you realize that nothing has ever stopped *her* heart except perhaps a surprise company dividend that is a direct product of her good work at the office. I can see our marriage all right, it would be an efficient partnership, but into that picture would never come her sudden joy as I walked out to join her again for a penthouse patio breakfast after a soft night of love. Ranya would be too busy swallowing the vast assortment of vitamins she takes every morning in order to keep herself right on top of commercial pressures.

However, she is a marvellous woman who has quite re-

vitalized Hok Lin Shipping. Board meetings used to be
me telling the other directors what I wanted; now they are
Ranya sparking ideas like a Siamese firecracker, some of
them with a real use potential, though I don't see why I
should have to marry her to keep these coming. At the
moment, though, it looks as though if I don't she'll chuck
Hok Lin and go back to running restaurants.

The bar started to fill, which meant that the last
veil had dropped, and there was post-erotic stimulus laughter around us of the kind which suggested that the lady had
hotted up the action towards her finale. I helped a slightly
elderly schoolteacher down off her stool without feeling
that we had missed much, and we went out on deck, walking the boards and staring at the mountains of China.

These didn't remind me of jungle-covered slopes down
in my home territory, they were bald, peeled as though
centuries ago anything once growing on them had been
stripped off to keep fires burning. A great many of China's
mountains have a nakedness that borders on the obscene,
old and wrinkled from weather gouging, and these were
bluish-grey, exactly the colour of a sea now affected by
sediment coming down the Pearl River.

'I'm booked into the Algarve Hotel,' Miss Jackson said.
'It's part of a package deal. Where are you staying?'

'There, too.'

'I hope it's as good as the brochures say. I'll admit to the
weakness of liking to be comfortable on my vacations. I
suppose that's what happens when you get older? Your
real spirit of adventure just dies.'

She chattered from a compulsion that hit her the
moment she was in contact with people again after her en-
durance contests with solitude. I felt uneasy. I don't enjoy
witnessing that terrible bustle, verbal or physical, which is
a product of loneliness; keep moving and you don't notice
it so much. It's like the only palliative for arthritis.

'Oh look, there they are again. I've been noticing them

ever since I got on board. You can't help it.'

'Who?'

'That young couple. They're so much in love.'

I turned. Miss Jackson was right, they were.

The girl and boy looked in their early twenties. They were walking hand in hand and China didn't interest them at all. Both were ash blond and though his hair was nearly as long as hers, resting on his shoulders, he didn't wear a beard or moustache, a lot of thought on this matter in front of a mirror had decided him that his face was far too beautiful to be screened. The girl was lovely, too. Their clothes were unisex, a symbolic expression of that total union of two souls and two bodies, tight-fitting slacks wide at the bottom, sleeveless thigh-length leather jackets with fringes, worn over mauve shirts open at the neck. The only real difference between them was height, and this appeared to trouble them a little, the boy with his head bent down, the girl's face lifted like a sunbathing addict's to the source of all real joy.

'See what I mean?' Miss Jackson said. 'Aren't they cute?'

I don't know whether or not the boy heard but he suddenly looked up, first at Miss Jackson, then at me, blue eyes that a moment before must have been very warm indeed now cooling, then going blank, establishing the generation gap like an earthquake fissure suddenly opened between their intense privacy and a world of squares. For just a fraction of a minute I didn't find that arrogance quite so cute and had to admonish myself. Here was the innocence that is so utterly vulnerable and inevitably so fleeting, and we all ought to salute it while it is still around. Miss Jackson looked as though she was remembering that first High School dance to which she had gone with the boy she had begun to think would never get up the nerve to invite her. Rosy recollection had peeled the years away, and I could see her as she must have been, breathless, eager and not a little frightened. What had happened to her romance? If I even prodded her gently she'd tell me.

We started to walk again and I realized almost at once that I had been firmly guided into doing this by Miss Jackson who wanted to keep Romeo and Juliet within vision. I didn't, so at the next flight of steps I took her arm just as firmly and more or less pushed her up to the boat deck. We sat down on a bench and soon found that phase one of our relationship had come to an end and momentarily we had nothing to talk about, even Miss Jackson. Phase two, of course, would be where we both started tentatively on our respective problems in living. I've had some terrible experiences in this area of human contact, including one pretty fresh in my mind from my last flight to England when I offered my window seat on the plane to an attractive woman in her middle thirties who refused this. I soon found out why, she wanted a captive audience. Within an hour after take-off she had laid out her life alongside our plastic feed trays, and that desperate need to use a total stranger had been almost unnerving. I couldn't pull down any personal reserve curtains, she would have snapped them up again. In a sense, too, I felt myself under attack, I was a man and a man had been the cause of her ruin. Also, there were marked similarities between me and that husband I got to know too well, we were both executive types in a frantically competitive world. Post-flight disorientation took me a lot longer than usual to get over on that trip. I never met the woman again, we didn't even have a drink at the airport after landing, but I can still see her face, dry-eyed, never a tear shed, she was long past that little relief.

A schoolteacher has long training in taking the initiative and Miss Jackson did this, reaching down into her carryall and producing a guidebook, flipping over its pages. I began to feel a bit like a not-too-bright student kept after school for some unpaid extra coaching, especially when she ran

her finger down a page and put the text firmly in my lap.
I was expected to read the indicated passage and did.
The guide was called *Your Six Weeks in the Far East*,
designed to make its publishers a fast buck from the new
tourism trend, and was candid about Macao as a sin-city
stop-over, suggesting at least a couple of nights to really
get the feel of the place.

'Many visitors to the Orient have never even heard
of Macao but, believe us, this tongue of land two and a
half miles long by one wide sticking out from Chairman
Mao's China is *well* worth a visit. Founded by the Portuguese in 1557, and long before the British claimed their
piece of territory only forty miles away, this little historical
anachronism is in marked contrast to bustling, frenetic
Hong Kong, from which it can be reached by hydrofoil
which does the trip in a little over an hour, or by slower
steamer, which lets you see the views. There is considerable new building along the waterfront, but behind and
around this is a town that seems to have its roots right
back in the seventeenth century, Portuguese colonial, with
brightly painted villas covering the small hills. There are
a few interesting historical ruins, the chief one the church
of St Paul, 1594-1602, whose façade was carved by Japanese Christians persecuted out of their homeland. The building was later destroyed by fire, though you can still see
the carvings. The poet Camoens did much of his best work
in a cave in the north part of the territory, apparently
because he couldn't afford a house. Streets tend to be
cobbled and there isn't a great traffic problem since you
can't really drive any place, the only road out of Macao
leads straight to China and a couple of soldiers keep you
from going through the gate.

'The main street, the Praya Grande, is within easy artil-
lery range from Red territory just across the water, and as
you walk along it you could well be in gun sights from over
there. In this setting is the Far East's Las Vegas, whatever

your game it is here waiting, and whatever your other pleasures they are delivered discreetly to your bedroom door (no matter how off-beat) as part of room service. All you have to do is ask and you can keep your voice down doing it. Prices are not yet Las Vegas's, but they are reaching for it. The US maintains a Consulate, but if you lose your shirt at the tables it is not a good idea to knock on that door for your two-dollar fare back to Hong Kong, you won't get it. A couple of major bank sub-offices used to be a better bet for the stranded but charity is growing thin there, too, so hold on to at least one of your travellers' cheques. The crime rate is low and you're unlikely to be knocked on the head in a dark lane even if you've had a big win.'

Lesson over I shut the book and handed it back. Miss Jackson dropped it into the carryall.

'I'm a bit disappointed in that guide,' she said. 'It seems awfully superficial.'

'Like contemporary travel.'

We both looked at China for a moment or two until she asked :

'You haven't told me what business you're in, Mr Harris?'

'Tramp steamers through Indonesia and a factory manufacturing marine diesel engines in Johore in Malaysia. I also own a small shipyard near Glasgow, in Scotland.'

'My goodness! You sound like a really big man.'

'Well, not all that big. The shipyard has run at a loss ever since I took it over and competition is threatening my tramps.'

'How about your engine factory?'

'That's doing all right at the moment but we only make two types and either, or both, could go out of fashion, which would mean a massive re-tooling I couldn't afford. So you see I have problems.'

'You make teaching school sound simple. And I often think how lucky we are with our summers off. Do you go off to all kinds of exciting places on your vacations?'

'The only time I took one I came back feeling terrible. My doctor said I was heading towards hypertension from trying to relax. He advised me not to risk it again, so I haven't!'

I could see that Miss Jackson wasn't quite certain when to take me seriously and in doubt she became brisk, so I was whipped off to the starboard rail to look at China again. A tiny pattern of houses was beginning to take shape on a promontory sticking out from mountains that hung over it like a frozen tidal wave. Those mountains belonged to Mao.

I'm not really as sold on the great thaw out here as the Pentagon and the British Foreign Office, this despite the fact that the change in political temperature has bene-fited me personally. Quite suddenly, after no purchase of my product for years, Peking decided that the bigger of my diesels was just what they needed for river junks and put in a sizeable order for it, this despite the fact that a Japan-ese trade delegation offering a rival engine was sitting right under their noses screaming at them not to touch mine. Maybe it was another case of oversell, like that soap powder campaign on television which drove irritated women to buy the brands which didn't promise to give them a ten per cent whiter wash. Certainly, I never went north to tout my product; the order came out of the blue to really brighten my week and spurt the small public issue of stock in the company by seventy-three cents. All this should have settled me right in at the heart of the new atmosphere of goodwill, and in a way it does, intellectually; at the same time I'm not joining the rush to view the treasures of the Summer Palace or go hiking along the Great Wall, I prefer conducting my business with the New China from neutral territory.

I do a good deal of this from Hong Kong, which offers reasonable personal security from a British-managed police force, though it is no place in which to leave any of your

company secrets lying about in an unlocked attaché case.
Anywhere in Hong Kong a thousand eyes are watching and
probably twice that number of ears, a lot of these mechanical, listening. The place is the headquarters Far East
for American, Russian, Chinese, Japanese, French and
British espionage services, as well as offering the world's
most sophisticated and comprehensive networks dealing
in commercial snooping, which means that a secret conference in a top-floor hotel suite is totally covered by half
a dozen agencies long before it starts. Macao, however,
from what I had heard of it, though strategically situated to
become a hotbed of intrigue of all kinds has apparently
kept itself pleasantly sleepy by sticking to pretty innocent
smuggling, the import of illegal gold, gambling and a
straightforward vice trade not yet controlled by international syndicates. There is no use bugging rooms from which
the only sound reaching tapes would be the snoring of
exhausted good-time people.

Miss Jackson and I watched a Portuguese colony begin
to take shape. Villas appeared as insets into green, not
quite as brightly coloured as the guidebook had suggested,
an original garishness now time-toned to merge with their
background. Three little hills were dotted with these houses
like pieces of contemporary chunky jewellery using the
semi-precious stones which don't really pretend to glitter.
I made out the church on high ground, just the front of it,
the rest a ruin, somehow reminding me of another conspicuous ruin, the cathedral in St Andrews in Scotland
which was destroyed not by the passage of centuries but
by the wild fury of one religious sect attacking the work
of another. Like St Paul's in Macao that Scottish shell
stands starkly symbolic of violence in the mind translated
into savage action. We keep forgetting that other ages have
seen plenty of this, too.

A ship's bell clanged. Our ferry began to slow from a
not very remarkable cruising speed as we ran into a shoal

of junks of all sizes, some with ribbed sails on twin masts set for the deep-sea fishing grounds, others only fifteen-footers propelled by stern cars. Even the smallest housed whole families under arches of canvas, with cooking pots and braziers squeezed on to tiny flat stern decks. This foreign territory, like a minute frill on the great mass of the continent, was still China, where space for man is at a premium and people are spilled over from land on to water to float out their living.

I had a look at some of the bigger ships. Macao isn't really a major port, and these were mostly coasters, but there was one considerably larger than the others, perhaps seven thousand tons. With a jolt of something like anger I recognized her funnel colours and the letters overprinted on them . . . OSL . . . which stood for Orient Shore Line. She was resting at the end of her anchor chain now but only ten days ago this tramp, the MV *Madoera,* had been down in the Java Sea, one of four OSL ships engaged in a ruthless price-cutting war against my company, Hok Lin. I was carrying a locked attaché case containing a dossier we had built up on Orient Shore Line activities since they started up two years earlier, and this included a photograph taken by Ranya of this particular ship leaving Semarang loaded with a cargo that should have been ours.

OSL were operating on a hit-and-run tactic, avoiding the smaller ports we visited, concentrating on the larger ones where there was a build-up of goods waiting to be lifted, suddenly pushing in one of their tramps to clean this out of dockside storage just before a scheduled visit by a Hok Lin ship. Actual contracts of long standing with us were being broken by shippers tempted by offers of ridiculously uneconomic freightage rates.

Over the last six months it had become completely obvious that this wasn't a general attack on the sea trade of the area, but beamed straight at us with the simple object of putting Hok Lin out of business, and at speed. Whoever was behind OSL knew perfectly well that we could not survive on our servicing of the smaller ports so had simply concentrated on hitting us where it would hurt most. A big hole in Hok Lin's trading profits for the year showed just how sound the OSL tactics were, a classic strategy which will always work if the attacker has the resources to sustain price-undercutting for an indefinite period. So far I hadn't a clue as to who was backing the new Macao-based company, this despite my expensive use of one of the best commercial espionage firms operating out of Hong Kong. All that I knew for certain was that big money was out to get me. I am unloved in a number of places, these including the skyscraper, earthquake-proofed head offices of a very large corporation in Tokyo.

The *Madoera* was having her superstructure repainted white, her owners able to afford to run her at a loss and still keep her looking fresh and successful. The glitter from those upper decks hurt my eyes. To rest them I looked down at the sampans, as Miss Jackson was doing. Some of the smallest seemed to be under magnetic attraction to our hull, coming very close to it, women at stern oars belabouring the water to prevent collisions.

'Mr Harris, why are they coming right in against us like this?'

'Watch and you'll see.'

We didn't have long to wait. The ferry's galley vent suddenly spurted out a flow of garbage. At once an old woman dropped her stern oar, picked up a butterfly net, slapped this into the water and dragged a load of waste to the side of her craft, hauling it up and emptying the dripping contents on stern deck boarding. Another woman emerged from under the hood and began to pick through the salvage.

'They're not going to . . . *eat* that?'

'Yes.'

'Oh no!'

It was a cry of pain. After months in Hong Kong she could still be shocked in a way that made her want to do something about what she saw. She belonged to a time when activist idealism was still acceptable and a girl could announce to the family that she was going to become a missionary without at once being seized and run in the Chrysler to the nearest psychiatrist to find out what had gone wrong with her sex life. I could almost see Miss Jackson striding through a north China mud village with an umbrella in one hand and a Gladstone bag in the other, this containing a bible covered over by a fairly comprehensive first-aid kit featuring disinfectants. Pre-Mao she would have made an effective servant of God and American hygiene.

She had turned away from the rail.

'Are those refugees down there?'

'I should think so. The lucky ones.'

'*Lucky* ones?'

'They've got hold of boats somehow. Most have nothing.'

'Isn't anything done for these people?'

'Probably quite a bit. But what your guidebook doesn't tell you is that nearly a third of Macao's population is made up of refugees. You can't do all that much.'

'Have you the same sort of situation down in Singapore?'

'No. Just unemployment.'

'And as a business man what do you do about that?'

'Carry a third more personnel on my payrolls than any management consultancy firm would say was economic.'

After a moment she asked : 'Are you uneconomic?'

'So far I've survived unrationalized,' I said. . . .

We docked next to the floating casino which might look exotic enough strung with lights at night but in the late afternoon showed rust stains. I would have thought that the daily boat could no longer be much of a thrill in a city now also served by a hydrofoil, but there was a big crowd on the jetty, as though strolling down to watch this routine arrival somehow put time's signature on another day. From a promenade deck Macao looked as pleasantly relaxed as the French Riviera must have done back in the days when Queen Victoria used to visit it, a nice getaway place for the rich which also had a sizeable population of natives offered the choice of serving their betters or quietly starving to death. But even here paradise wasn't going to last, the portents of change obvious, a gaming ship and new hotels for mass tourism.

Customs were merely the gesture one might expect where the big industry is smuggling, and when we were through them Miss Jackson, in a brooding mood, no longer interested in youth and beauty, agreed with my suggestion that we walk to our hotel. We gave the luggage to a Macanese taxi-driver with a sizeable strain of Portuguese in his blood lines, and set off, past a row of parked cars. One of these stuck out a long way beyond the Fiat and Morris flanking it, a shining, new, lemon-coloured Cadillac. It is not a car you see very often in the Orient where the status symbol for those who have made it tends to be the Mercedes, but in Malaysia I had known one Chinese who had a weakness for this make amounting to an addiction, trading in his old one for the latest model every year. Teng Ching Wok, suddenly wanted by the police in at least two countries, had fled to Macao in some haste, and presumably still with access to a numbered account in a Swiss bank, the kind of refugee the colony caters for rather better than it does for those other Chinese who have to swim to sanctuary, arriving empty-handed.

I stared at that car. It seemed inconceivable that anyone other than Teng would want anything as big for use in a territory only six miles square. Then, while I was still staring, a man broke from the line of stragglers ahead of us.

He was wearing jeans and a bright shirt and carrying a small wooden case which he set down behind the Cadillac while he used a key on its vast stern overhang. The lid sprang up, he lifted the case, slid it in and slammed the lid down, turning towards us. I recognized him immediately, you do someone who has once tried to kill you. His name was Ho Tai and he was Teng Ching Wok's private gorilla.

CHAPTER II

For anyone whose basic travel experience has to be the Turkestan Hilton or the Galapagos Sheraton the Algarve Hotel in Macao would be dead right. My air-conditioned bedsitter with a button-control panel for everything didn't have a balcony but it did have louvered blinds of a kind I hadn't seen before and when I asked the porter who brought up my bags about these he explained, in Latinized English, that the really happy people in this city play all night and sleep by day. The unique shutters had been fitted to keep out the offensive light. That's one up on Las Vegas, but aside from a single unusual feature everything felt safe enough and you could make your sorties into strangeness from this tower certain that when you got back to it, and if you didn't look too closely at the elevator boy, you might never have left Cincinnati.

I tried out the room service which the guidebook had recommended so highly, a first test that might look easy, but wasn't asking for a bottle of twelve-year-old Glen Grant, expecting that if they had the malt in stock it would be the five-year-old. But it wasn't, my whisky was delivered by a dark, smiling Macanese youth who looked as though his work here was nothing but a succession of fat tips and when I saw the red overprinting on the label I gave him fifty escudos. His grin widened and he bowed three times as he half backed towards the door, so I knew we were friends.

I allowed myself a fair ration to unpack with and after putting things in drawers moved the window louvers slightly until they took in the view to the north of mountains which didn't belong to Portugal. There is actually some doubt that the city beneath me belongs to Portugal for the lease is fluid and administrators from Lisbon never do anything that could possibly irritate the landlord up in Peking. And that is where Teng Ching Wok's bosses lived. They had been his bosses during his whole time in Malaysia while he was pretending to be a neutralist tycoon with his stake in the country to which his grandfather had emigrated. When all that had quite suddenly collapsed about his ears flight to this city had been inevitable, Macao being the only feather bed available for failed undercover Communists who want to go on owning big American limousines. It could be argued that Peking allows Macao to continue to exist as a colony just to have it handy as a retreat for all Marxist millionaires exposed by mission failures. Russia could do with a little enclave of a similar kind somewhere along the shores of the Mediterranean as a recruitment incentive. A villa in the Crimea with three servants and a Ziz executive model just isn't a big enough inducement, it is too far from your old friends. All the boys who have opted for that when they had to run would now, I'm sure, if they were honest, admit that Russia is a lonely place for foreigners even if ex-top spies do eventually get buried in a niche in the Kremlin Wall. Who wants to put in waiting time in the Crimea for that kind of immortality?

But Macao is utterly different. Here is a nicely concentrated distillation of the world's delights with the source of your basic inspiration just down the road if you need it, while at the same time you live immune from your spiritual motherland's physical austerities.

I wondered if Teng suffered from claustrophobia sometimes on his tiny peninsula? He just might risk a little cautious travel away from it now and again on a false passport but I had the feeling that head office would frown on too much of this. Certainly he could never re-visit his old haunts down south. In Malaysia the warrant for his arrest remained permanently available and in Singapore my old friend Chief Superintendent Kang would lock Teng up in Changi Jail, leaving him there for some years with his case pending, which was exactly what the scoundrel rated.

I was having dinner with Miss Jackson, which was inevitable, and the hotel brochure had already told me that I would be sampling the featured African spiced chicken and drinking a little Mateus with it. A number of restaurants almost certainly owned by the management were also mentioned, but these weren't for our first night, we'd play safe where we could be certain to get glasses of ice water with the prawn cocktail and American coffee. After that we might risk the casino, just to watch. Somehow I wasn't looking forward to it.

We met in the foyer. Miss Jackson was wearing a near cocktail dress that might have been chosen by a welfare worker who didn't go in for much frivolity but every now and then had to appear on a lecture platform. It was safe. She was also wearing a family heirloom Victorian brooch on one shoulder which was pretty, and carried a black handbag large enough to hold that guidebook. We were given a table near an air-conditioning vent and the temperature was practically sub-arctic. She talked about world hunger while all around us was loud chatter in assorted languages about lucky runs at the gaming tables. I didn't say much, which suited my companion who was practically working out a thesis verbally. She must have been a very good-looking girl but I was beginning to see why males had been scared off, these facing the prospect of a lifetime, or at least long years until Reno, with an acute social consciousness that began to function even before breakfast. For all the empathy achieved between us Miss Jackson could be exhausting.

Our investigation of the gambling didn't take us as far as the ship, only to the hotel's own casino built out at the back as an annex and to which the public had direct access from a side road. The public certainly used the place, it was humming, the crowd a mix of tourists and locals. There didn't seem to be any prohibitions about admitting children, kids ran about while their mums lost the house-keeping money. The percentage of females was high, old Chinese women in dark blue with black hair pulled tight to buns, who might have come straight across the Praya Grande from their sampans and young Chinese women in cheongsams showing a great deal of thigh. A few of the male tourists were in dinner jackets, but not many, the atmosphere highly informal. Cries of croupiers mixed with the clank of fruit machine handles coming down and under all this was a steady drone from taped music. We moved amongst the tables looking for someone Lady Luck had touched on the shoulder to grant a wild winning streak but it appeared that the lady was away from Macao. There were plenty of tense faces but none joyous. It was too early for the real professionals who are interesting to the extent that they never show any feeling at all and watching this lot was about as exciting as staring at a bridge game when you don't play yourself.

'Mr Harris, if you'll excuse me, I think I'll just go early to bed tonight.'

'Good idea. I'll do the same.'

In the box going up she said:

'I suppose you'll be busy tomorrow?'

'During the morning at any rate. I'm not quite sure what my day will bring.'

She nodded, accepting again the familiar prospect of solitude.

'I thought I'd just sort of mosey around. I guess there's not much problem in doing that in this town, you ought to be able to walk anywhere. That's useful when you're saving pennies. I might take a picture of that gate into China. It ought to be something to remember.'

In the corridor outside her room it seemed to me she looked pale.

'Are you feeling all right, Miss Jackson?'

'Just a little tired, that's all. I'll admit I can't quite get out of my mind that woman with the butterfly net.'

'Is that why you didn't eat much at dinner?'

'Well, maybe.'

'Don't let what you saw keep you awake. The sampan woman could be down in that casino now.'

She looked at me with a tight little smile.

'Good night, Mr Harris.'

I went up two floors cursing myself for the cynicism, yet knowing it might well be the truth. Outside of the new China all Chinese gamble. It is more important to them than food, and food is more important than sex.

The bottle of malt welcomed me. I accepted the invitation, then moved over with my glass to a fitted chest, unlocking the second drawer down with a key I had been carrying around in my pocket. When you suspect that your possessions may be searched, and I tend to suspect this quite often while travelling, it is a good idea to create a strong impression in your room of personal untidiness. The searcher is then not going to bother too much about leaving things neat when he has finished his work. Hotel maids don't usually probe into locked drawers but someone had been in this one while I was out. It contained, partially covering my attaché case, a sweater, some shirts, socks and handkerchiefs, the chaos arranged in a standard pattern I evolved long ago, this basically a couple of socks a third of the way up on to the black leather in a kind of V. Now they weren't even on the leather, and my opening of the drawer couldn't have knocked them off. Even the sweater wasn't quite as I had left it.

The key, like the lock it fitted, was mass produced and probably standard to all the bedrooms, which ruled in a maid again, but she could be a girl with a special mission. I lifted out the attaché case and had a close look at the lock holding down the flap. This hadn't been forced, but the shiny chrome bore faint traces of new scratching. Nothing inside was missing, my briefing for this trip just as I had inserted it, eleven typed pages on all we had un-covered so far about the activities of Orient Shore Line, some of these verging on the criminal. Ranya's photo-graph of the *Madoera* was there, too, but I knew that none of this was any longer confidential, my visitor would almost certainly have brought along a microcamera with built in flash, practically standard snooping equipment these days. It was just as well that the only really useful evidence I had against OSL was a letter kept in my wallet.

I will admit to a certain prejudice against lawyers, though I'm not suggesting for one minute that the great majority of these gentlemen don't conduct their professional affairs with the strictest probity. It is just that I seem to have been unlucky, coming up against the mavericks who cheer-fully take two per cent of a total estate as their fee for half a day's work preparing a simple will for probate. Ramundo P. Alvares looked as though his usual charge for this little service would be five per cent.

I had rung him for an appointment and he hadn't seemed at all keen to let me have one until I made noises suggesting that I was far enough off balance mentally to be contemplating litigation which could go on for years, paying for all the running costs on his mistress while it did. He fixed our meeting for twelve noon.

My taxi had taken me along the Praya before turning up into a twisting shopping street that was making its living out of pretending to be a piece of old Portugal, cobbles and all. From this we had progressed to a very charming plaza full of stone arches and with a fountain in the middle, but marred on its northern side by five floors of concrete and glass. In this Señor Alvares had his offices, contemporary, cool, furnished with flat veneered surfaces and armless chairs mounted on curved steel, not a hint anywhere of big black boxes containing the documents of family estates or any of that casual clutter of deed-covered desks which distressed widows appear to find so comforting. Here even the typewriters were silent electric, manned by groomed Macanese girls who looked as though they wouldn't be in the least homesick holding down a job in Manhattan.

I was offered a Manila cigar which I accepted and a glass of iced rosé which I refused, and for the first ten minutes Ramundo vetted me carefully in a gentle, but rich vibrato. I told him my Hong Kong contacts had recommended him as Macao's most with-it solicitor, though what had actually been said over a quick drink in a Kowloon bar was that if I wanted someone with a finger in every local pie Ramundo was the man to go to but in any dealings with him I was to keep a sharp lookout for trip wires. From his side he declared no interest in or any dealings with Orient Shore Lines in Macao and on the strength of this statement I handed over an eleven-page document, no longer confidential, for him to read.

While he did this I had a good look at him. He was hirsute and could have screened his face with a luxuriant beard and moustaches but had decided to go unmasked in his dealings with clients, compromising with ear coverings of long, wavy, pomaded black hair. One look told you his favourite sport was women as it usually is with husky-voiced males who carry dark fur on the backs of their hands. I put him in the late thirties somewhere and he had already come a long way along an increasingly attractive road. It would take a considerable shock to crack his urbanity.

When he had finished the last page of my notes Alvares readjusted the clip holding them to his satisfaction, then put the sheets down on a stretch of clean blotting paper. He reached for his rosé which he sipped thoughtfully while he considered his opening gambit. His English was good, learned as the necessary lingua franca of contemporary affairs, almost without accent.

'Mr Harris, is this meant to be a précis of your contemplated case against Orient Shore Line?'

'In a way.'

'But you hint here at evidence. Have you anything positive to offer?'

'At the moment just one letter from a merchant in Pontianak explaining, over his signature, how he had been blackmailed into shipping with OSL after contracting with Hok Lin.'

'May I see this letter?'

'It will be available after you have agreed to take the case.'

'I see. One letter only?'

'I'm quite sure that when the action I mean to take is known I will be able to get signed and witnessed statements from a number of other merchants saying that they were coerced by threats against person and property to transfer to OSL ships goods which had already been contracted to my ships.'

'When you say contracted do you mean that these agreements were verbal through your local agents or in writing to your Singapore office?'

'I have letters from these merchants specifying the goods to be shipped and stating that these were already warehoused waiting for our next call at their ports. Couldn't these be interpreted as a binding contract?'

Alvares should have called me a fool then, but he didn't.

'That's something I'll have to consider.'

I didn't have to consider it for one minute, there wasn't a hope of any court in any country interpreting a written expression of intent as a binding legal contract.

'This violence you mention, Mr Harris, is there any case of it actually happening?'

'It hasn't happened yet. It could at any time.'

'What you are saying is that to date there have only been these threats?'

'Yes.'

'What form did they take?'

'Anonymous telephone calls.'

'I see.'

He was working hard to keep contempt for me out of his expression.

'Mr Alvares, those telephone calls have to be considered in the light of conditions prevailing in Indonesia where the Chinese merchant is still far from popular, even under the new regime. Under the old one, as you'll remember, they were expelled in great numbers, and in circumstances very like that of the Asians from Uganda. The traders who survived those times live in fear of another pogrom against them. Rightly or wrongly they believe that, if it came to real trouble, they wouldn't get much help from the Indonesian police. That's why those phone calls mean so much more than they would most places, they come from the heart of that fear in which these people live all the time.'

The lawyer gave respectful attention to my little sermonette, the price for doing this later to be added to my account. He leaned back in his chair and put the tips of his fingers together.

'Just what kind of legal action had you in mind, Mr Harris?'

It was plain now that prolonged litigation was out, a great disappointment to him.

'I want an injunction from a court in Macao against a company registered here restraining that company from future menaces against my customers in Indonesia.'

He said something half under his breath in Portuguese, obviously disturbed by my proposition. He cleared his throat so that his voice became slightly less husky.

'And what would be the practical purpose of such an injunction?'

'Publicity,' I said.

'*What?*'

His hands fell out of that ecclesiastical pose. I leaned forward.

'Look, Mr Alvares, I'll fight a price-cutting war by matched price-cutting and without yelling for help to anyone. But intimidating my customers is quite another matter. I've got to find a different way to fight that. And publicity is the way. A court injunction against OSL would get in the papers. This would mean a lot of sympathy for me over a wide area, here in this city, in Hong Kong, Singapore, wherever Chinese business is predominant. Though Hok Lin is not strictly a Chinese company any more the people involved in this with me are Chinese working against considerable odds. I know how to make use of publicity, and I have a new co-director, a lady, who gets on very well with the Press. We've already found this remarkably useful and I can promise you that if we get that injunction from a Macanese court we'd be giving some interesting press conferences. There is no doubt at all that my colleague, Mrs Nivalahannanda will do an excellent job of interesting the news media. OSL would be in the limelight. I believe that not only would they stop menacing customers but that the people behind this would be greatly disturbed by that glare down on them. There's a fair chance that they might call off their operations against me by their proxy company.'

Alvares was now staring.

'*Proxy* company?'

'Of course. Some big interests are trying to get at me through a phoney little company with four ships that couldn't begin to operate at the huge loss it must be taking unless there is big money behind them. The big white light of news interest is the last thing these people want, which is why I'm going to see that it's switched on. If you can get me that injunction I want from a Macao court I'll pay you twenty-five thousand US dollars. Into a Swiss bank if you prefer that arrangement.'

Professional ethics should have made the lawyer indignant but instead of throwing me out of his office he got up and went over to the windows to look out on the square this building had ruined, standing with his back turned, hairy hands clasped behind it. Twenty-five thousand dollars is a lot of money and I was prepared to up that figure since I was perfectly certain that I would never be called upon to pay it.

'My offer, of course, Mr Alvares, is on that tug company formula, "no cure, no pay".'

He turned.

'Am I to understand that you mean if I don't get that injunction I have no claim on a professional fee?'

'That's right.'

'It's a most unusual proposition to put to a man in my profession.'

'It's a most unusually large fee.'

A glare from the windows was behind him and I couldn't see his expression.

'If you don't get this injunction what will you do?'

'Use other means to focus down publicity on OSL. This won't be as good as an injunction but I have one or two ideas that might work very well. You'll appreciate, of course, that I would much prefer to have the majesty of the

C

law behind me. Which is why I'm in Macao.'

Alvares came back to his seat and sat down again. He picked up my sheets.

'May I keep this?'

'I think it would be better if I did at the moment.'

He handed them over, watching me fit them into my case. Then he said judicially:

'I'll need a little time to consider this matter, Mr Harris. How long are you staying here?'

'As long as is necessary.'

'In that case I'll be in touch with you as soon as possible.'

I accepted dismissal and stood. We shook hands across the broad desk. On the way to the door I turned.

'By the way, I understand you bought a property here some years ago for a friend of mine.'

'Oh? Who would that be?'

'Teng Ching Wok.'

Lawyers rarely permit themselves to react as though a low voltage current had suddenly reached them through their chair but Alvares's body positively jerked.

'A bit of a recluse now,' I said. 'Well, no doubt he has his reasons for that.'

The Macanese secretaries in the outer office looked cool and bored but I didn't think the man I had just left was either of these things.

I lunched off a tray in my hotel room, sitting at the windows looking at the mountains of China. I had first seen these in the late afternoon and at dusk when they were heavily emphasized by shadow and I suppose I had been expecting hard sunlight to push them back a bit, making them less bullying, but it didn't. At night a fair percentage of the lights had come from Communist windows but then you couldn't draw any line of demarcation, Marxist electric bulbs apparently as good as capitalist ones. Now the drawn lines were there, the most conspicuous being a long row of floating buoys marking the end of Portuguese territorial waters. The MV *Madoera* was anchored well beyond these, at least a couple of miles away in the lee of what could only be a Chinese island, this presumably because she drew too much water to enter the harbour, which has a silt problem. It is that silt coming from the many mouths of a huge river which has always kept Macao from becoming a port that could even begin to rival Hong Kong, and now made it an odd choice as the headquarters of a relatively new shipping company.

The Praya Grande was almost deserted under full heat and I decided to share the siesta the natives were enjoying, suddenly sleepy from a bottle of beer. The phone bell woke me. I looked at my watch, twenty past four.

'Paul Harris here.'

I heard the caller's breathing before his voice, quite a loud wheeze.

'Teng Ching Wok.'

'Well! This is interesting. I wondered if you'd get in touch. Ho Tai told you I'd arrived?'

'Yes.'

'I've often wondered what happened to him. You find him useful up here, too?'

There was that wheezing again, almost asthmatic.

'Paul . . . what happened . . . years ago . . . was nothing personal.'

'Oh, I realized that. I don't bear malice, Teng. At least not much. You were only doing your political duty.'

'I was under pressures!'

'Of course. We all are.'

'You got in the way. There was nothing I could do.'

'Teng, don't go on about it. It's ancient history.'

'Does that mean . . . you're willing to forget?'

'Well, not exactly. There are some things you never quite forget.'

'I can tell you this, I've been troubled ever since.'

He certainly wasn't sounding like his old self at all.

'You mean you've been kept awake nights? You'll have me in tears in a minute.'

'This isn't funny!'

'I didn't think it was funny either, having Ho Tai padding after me in that bloody park with his strangler's hands at the ready. And he still looks in pretty good shape.'

'Ho Tai's just my servant, that's all.'

'A couple of refugees together. You knew that I left Kuala Lumpur not long after your people burned down my house?'

'Yes. But they're not my people, Paul, I swear it! Not any longer.'

'You mean you've given up politics?'

'I'm a sick man.'

'Sorry to hear that. So you've really retired?'

'I can't get about any more. I don't try to. I just stay in my house. Would you come here?'

'On one condition.'

'What's that?'

'I don't see Ho Tai.'

'You won't, I promise. How about tonight? Say seven for a drink?'

No invitation to dinner. I would have thought that the least you could do for a man you had tried to murder was feed him well as part of the reconciliation.

'All right,' I said. 'How do I get to you?'

'I'll send a car.'

'Fine.'

'Paul, have you brought a secretary? That woman with you?'

'A tourist. We met on the ferry. I have to be back here at least by nine tonight to take a call from Singapore. I'll arrange to have it relayed to your number if we find we have so much to catch up on. Are you in the book?'

'There's no need to cover yourself! I tell you I . . .'

'See you at seven.'

I hung up, and with the feeling that my host this evening would give a great deal not to have to entertain me. Teng might be a sick man but he hadn't retired from the action.

I didn't rate the Cadillac, the car calling for me at quarter to seven, an ordinary taxi with an ordinary driver. Perhaps this was because Ho Tai was the only one who could manœuvre that great monster through the narrow streets. It was a slow enough ride even in the taxi over cobbles flanked by pleasantly mouldering buildings with arched façades with pitch black lanes going off between them. The road lighting wasn't brilliant which put the accent on patches of brightness, most of these appearing to be guidebook restaurants sending out eddies of human noise and spicing the hot, still air with food smells.

Then came suburbs on rising ground, these pretty old Portugal, high walls, grilled gates, and dark masses of lush growth glimpsed briefly. Every now and then headlights picked up baskets of flowers just hanging from pegs driven into stonework, householders making the gesture of decorating their town while at the same time maintaining a strict, almost totally burglar-proof privacy behind massive ramparts. A few houses did present a gable end to the twisting street, this usually an upsurge of the garden wall with, very high, a one-barred window. There was money up here and had been for centuries, once Portuguese money but now probably adhering to a selection of émigrés from all corners of the globe busily engaged in equally eccentric ways of earning it. I had heard that some of the residents even commuted to Hong Kong daily.

We stopped and I got out. I didn't tip the driver and he left me to continue on up the hill, tail lights disappearing. I stood in a patch of light borrowed from a garden in which there was a highly artistic arrangement of concealed spots shining on palms and splashes of flower colour which included a bed of cannas. A flagstoned path wound away into mystery, the house completely invisible and a barred gate filling its stone arch had wrought-iron decoration, large blooms and leaves. I put my hand on one of the rods supporting this trimming to feel cold steel. The gate had no handle. To gain admission into this fortress you pulled an antique chain heavy enough to ring a huge bronze bell and waited.

I had a long wait and during it was quite certain I was being inspected by close-circuit television. Then there was a click, grilling swung back and I went in. Reception was a little eerie. Electronic security devices should be humanized by a voice from a speaker set behind a plumbago saying : 'Welcome, friends.' All I heard was the click of the grille securing itself again.

The flagstones became steps and at the top of these was a hibiscus hedge high enough for a maze which went on for yards. I came around the end of this to see an S-shaped swimming-pool tinted blue by underwater bulbs The surrounds had wooden Japanese lanterns up on poles, all lit, and overhanging the pool, half obscuring the house beyond it, was a massive terrace of piled-up stone reached by a flight of flower-garlanded steps. Teng Ching Wok wasn't paying for all this on his pension from Peking.

My host was waiting for me seated in a Hong Kong wicker chair. After all that brightness down below the terrace seemed dark, a huge expanse of paving lit only by a weirdly coloured fountain spouting three jets and, at some distance, table lamps beyond the glass wall of a living-room. There was a chair for me and next to it a drinks trolley. This reunion wasn't going to allow us to see much of each other.

'Forgive me not getting up, Paul.'

'That's all right. What's this place called?'

'Villa Setubal.'

'Beautiful.'

It was, too, the creation of a man who doesn't believe

there is any place you can take anything after you've gone.
Most of Macao was in the view together with a nice
selection of Communist-lit windows across water. The
mountains cut off stars like a thick, black wavering brush
stroke.

'I thought we'd stay out here. Unless the occasional
mosquito bothers you?'

'Not at all.'

'Then sit down and help yourself to a drink. I think
everything's there.'

I had to peer at the bottles, not finding a malt, just
the gilded label of what claims to be the world's best scotch
whisky and isn't, but is still quite drinkable watered. In
a chair with a high back between him and available
light Teng was not much more than a bulk with a white
splash of face.

'You don't seem to have a glass,' I said. 'Can I pour
yours?'

'Tonic water, no ice.'

'What?'

'I can't touch alcohol. Liver condition.'

'That sounds bad.'

'It's hell. I told you I'm ill.'

'When did this start?'

'About a year ago.'

You make yourself a paradise and a history of over-
indulgence catches up. I was getting used to the dim out
and could see him better. He had always been overweight
but now he was fat and that whiteness of face seemed to
be sagging down on to his shoulders. His voice had changed,
too, holding the authentic whine of the chronic invalid who
is bitter about his state. When he leaned forward to take
his glass he gave a little grunt. There was a considerable
silence after he had rustled himself back again into that
wicker nest, as though he found it difficult to get a social
conversation going. He was like an actor whose mind has

gone blank, waiting in desperation for aid from the
prompt corner. Then, as though that voice from behind
a curtain had come, he started off on the right tack, refugee
nostalgia.

Some of this was probably perfectly real, Malaysia had
been his home and he had certainly been working hard
down there for the kind of Malaysia he wanted, which
was the exact opposite of the one I wanted. But nothing
political came into Teng's flow, he was almost an elderly
gent maundering on about an idealized yesterday and
though I didn't get much from all this I did get one
thing, he hated Macao, the beautiful Villa Setubal was
his prison because beyond that grille into a quiet street
was a world that menaced him now. Behind its Portuguese
façade this city might be under the complete control of
the people he had served but this didn't offer the refugees
any real security. There was that hydrofoil to Hong Kong
and the ferry and men like me could come in quietly, apparently for the gaming. One of Chief Superintendent Kang's
men from Singapore could also come in and as Teng knew
well the Chief Superintendent was no ordinary policeman
operating solely within the bounds of his official jurisdiction.
He had been operating outside of it when he had nearly
caught Teng.

I didn't have much talking to do, every now and then
providing a cue line which was all that was needed to
set my host off again. He even got down to personal remin-
iscence, to laughter shared, and I longed to point out,
though I didn't, that whatever had been between us once
had been killed stone dead because it had been based, at
least partially, on sham from his side. Like a fool I had
taken friendship at face value and there must have been
many times when he laughed at me because of this.
I was being softened up now, for what I could only guess,
but one thing was obvious, Teng had lost subtlety in his
isolation, he wasn't able to deal easily with people any

more and under all this gabble was a continuing nervousness.

A girl arrived with a tray of small eats which she slid on to the lower level of the trolley, at once dismissed by Teng in Cantonese. I turned my head but only got a back view of a trouser suit in drab brown. She might be a servant or one of his women, he had always kept his women in the background and I couldn't remember ever having been introduced to one of his wives.

'Help yourself, Paul. There are cigars down there, too. You haven't told me yet what brought you to Macao?'

'I thought Alvares would have done that?'

The big chair creaked, then a silence in marked contrast to three quarters of an hour of garrulity. When he did speak it was as though he was having to squeeze the words out.

'I . . . don't understand?'

'Isn't he your lawyer?'

'I've used him, yes.'

'Which was what I was trying to do. I had a tip off that he might well be my best lead to Orient Shore Line's man in Macao.'

'Paul, what are you talking about?'

'If you don't know then I've been following a false lead. I'm in Macao to find out who are backing OSL. I'm not interested in that chairman and managing director named on the company notepaper. They've been vetted. They're nobodies. I didn't think a visit to the so-called head office here would do me much good, either. But I did feel that after my session with Alvares there was a very good chance that the real local agent of OSL would get in touch with me first. And you rang.'

'My God, just because I ring you up . . . !'

'And with a pretty phoney line in remorse, Teng. Slightly worse than that babble you've just finished turning out.'

'This is . . . crazy!'

'You protest too loudly. You still claim you know nothing about OSL?'

'All I know is that it operates out of Macao. I sometimes see their ships down there.'

'Your monastery offers you a god's eye view? Is that all you do these days, just sit here staring down?'

'Yes.'

'I don't believe it. Your assets were in that Malaysian town you practically owned. You ran about nine businesses in the place. That's where your money was and you had to leave fast. With no one forwarding the take from the sell-up auctions. If you'd been an outstanding success as an undercover Marxist I might be able to see Peking making you as comfortable as this, but you weren't. You were a flop. Peking hates a flop. And they're also mean about spending foreign currency. I'm damn certain you still have to work to keep all this going.'

'You came here . . . just to throw all this at me?'

'Why else would I come?'

He dropped his glass then. I don't know whether it was shock or just a diversion to give himself time to establish a better defensive position, but the thing certainly shattered, leaving some nasty jagged bits about our feet lying there catching the faint light. I didn't try to pick them up.

'Teng, I've another reason for being in Macao besides finding out who is behind a proxy company and that is to learn why I'm important enough for anyone to want to bankrupt me.'

'Do I have to go on telling you I know nothing about all this?'

'I'd say you were a natural for the appointment as local director of this operation against Hok Lin. You knew me well, how I worked, my connections in Malaysia, all those little things which go towards rounding out an inquiry service report. And you were redundant, written off by China as a liability, needing money. You'd take the

job, any job in which your Marxist background didn't
trouble your principals. Well, I've a message for you to
deliver to those principals. It's this . . . I'll spend every
penny I have fighting the bastards. And they needn't
think they'll be able to go on hiding behind that OSL
screen, there are some bad rips in it already.'

I got up. He was a big flaccid shape in the chair. One of
my shoes crunched on glass.

'Have your goon open the gate,' I said. 'I've got to get
back to take that call from Singapore. I'll tell Chief Superintendent Kang you send your love. He'll like that. He
hasn't forgotten you.'

It may have been anger, I don't know, but by the time
I reached the north end of the Praya on foot and smelled
cooking from night stalls I was wildly hungry. I went over
to have a look and found one old woman ladling out
curried prawns into blue and white bowls with customers
queueing up. When you see Chinese in a line for a meal you
are usually all right, and I tacked myself on at the end.
After about five minutes, with my stomach grumbling at
the delay, I got my portion and stood pushing it down
with chopsticks in the light from acetylene flares. I had a
refill and then a bowl of steaming rice, moving on to another
canvas-sided shack for green tea and paper thin salty wafers.
After that I walked along the Praya Grande getting back
into the bright world of casino lights and a general emphasis
on night living.

Another old Chinese woman was selling flowers, tight
little bunches with the colour drained out of them by
street lamps. She was in patched blue, no ornaments at
all, not a hint of jade, which meant real poverty. An en-
durance contest with life had gouged her face. She wanted
fifteen escudos for her flowers but when I gave her ten
was quite pleased that she had cheated me. I went on
looking for some place where I could ditch the posy but

there was no shadow at all except small patches cast by palm trees. These, with the lighting, made this avenue look like imitation Miami. All that was needed was a few more pre-fabricated hotels and they would come.

The car which came to a stop by the kerb twenty yards ahead had squealing brakes. Then there was other squealing, human and very loud. A back door was open and someone was being pushed through it, but resisting this. I didn't see it was a girl until she suddenly broke free, standing on the pavement, but she couldn't have been escaping for she returned to the attack, arms flailing out at someone in the back seat, her noise a mix between lamentation and fury. Then she was given a heavy push and went backwards into the trunk of a palm, sliding slowly down this, still looking towards the car and still screaming. The car drove off.

There were people nearer the girl than I was. A youth stopped to look down at her, then decided he wasn't a Samaritan and moved on. The girl stopped screaming, sitting on the circle of earth under the palm, propped against the trunk, beginning to hiccup. I said in Cantonese:

'Are you hurt?'

She looked up. Black from eye make-up was smudged down one cheek. She lifted a hand to find an ear-ring missing, rolled over and began to crawl on paving stones looking for it. Strollers stopped but when the girl pushed herself up and stood swaying they moved on, leaving the situation to me, as though they didn't much like the look of her. She turned quite slowly to stare, her eyes starting at my feet, working up. She seemed to focus for quite some time on that bunch of flowers, then her head jerked back and she started to scream again:

'Two of them! They used me and didn't pay! Foreigners!'

Suddenly she came at me, her hands up. I saw the bright red of her fingernails.

CHAPTER III

The guidebooks simply don't give you a hint about what to do in a situation like this. My reaction was on the slow side, I grabbed a wrist but the girl's free hand was dangerously near my right eye before I knocked it away. We trampled flowers. I smelled a mix of bazaar perfume and garlic. She spat words in my face, none of them pretty, while we wrestled. Then she broke free and went back to the palm, leaning on it, a grotesque parody of invitation. A tourist walking alone on the Praya was being mocked.

'You want to come to my boat, foreigner? It's just over there.'

'No thanks.'

'You think I'm too dirty?'

I started off up the pavement. She shouted:

'Maybe you'd like my brother? He's fourteen. Just right.'

She laughed. The sound of that followed me for quite some time. I wanted a drink.

The foyer clock said quarter to nine and the hotel was humming. I went into the bar which was almost as dark as they keep these places in New York and it was a minute or two before I could really see anything. Voices came from the blacked-out booths but most of the stools up at the counter were empty and I sat on one of them, served my whisky at once by a Macanese Eurasian youth who looked as though his experience of life had already killed all his small talk. When he wasn't getting drinks he polished glasses, gazing at the floor as he did it. It must have been ten minutes later when the stool next to mine was taken. An American voice ordered whisky. I turned my head to see fair hair reaching down to the stiff, wide upturned collar of a floral shirt. It was Romeo from the ferry, but without his girl. He sat slumped forward over the counter and though it was a remarkable profile he was slightly less beautiful tonight, perhaps because his mouth stayed open, as though he found it easier to breathe that way. He got out a pack of cigarettes, using a gold lighter, a ring glinting. Then he looked at me, quite a long look.

'Hallo,' he said.

The greeting was half belligerent, not really a bridge thrown out across the gap between two solitaries. I nodded, fumbling in a trouser pocket to get change for another drink. He watched me putting the money down on the counter and then it being taken away by the barman.

'What the hell do you do in this town if you don't gamble?'

Since he had a girl the answer seemed obvious.

'Go to bed.'

'That's what I thought,' he said, sour. 'What if I don't want to?'

'Then you're in a bad way.'

'Sure. That's me.'

He thought about himself, staring at his glass.

'You English?'

'Scots.'

'Same thing, isn't it?'

'No.'

'What you got in Scotland that's so special?'

'A lot fewer people to the square mile.'

'Well, that's something. Hell, that's something. You know where I've been this last year? Hong Kong. Too many damn people. Millions. All dancing on the head of a pin.'

'Are you in business out here?'

'No, I'm not in business out here. I'm a hangover.'

'From what?'

'The Peace Corps.'

'How do you become a hangover from that?'

'By not knowing when it's time to go home.'

'Where do you live in the States?'

'Dayton, Ohio. Too many people there, too. We keep breeding. That's what I want to do. A lot of kids. An eight-roomed house.'

'There are worse things.'

'Not these days, man. The trouble with me is I'm a throwback. I'm the new thing and that's a throwback.'

'I don't follow?'

'I just found out. I'm a Nixon conservative. Isn't that a helluva thing to find out about yourself?'

'If your girl is a Nixon conservative, too, you ought to be able to work things out.'

'You saw us or something?'

'On the ferry. You stood out from the crowd.'

'How?'

'You looked happy.'

'God! That was yesterday. My girl's not a conservative. She's a hopper.'

'What's that?'

'Grasshops. One country to the other. Valparaiso. Madras. You name it, she goes there. So long as it's not the States. She spits on the States. When I say Dayton, Ohio, she makes a gargling noise.'

'Does it have to be Dayton?'

'It does. We've got a family car business there. And my total qualifications fit me for selling cars. The United American Federation of Automobile agents' annual convention in Miami. How about that?'

'Can I buy you a drink?'

'No. When I'm drunk I buy my own drinks. And I'm drunk. You've lived, man, how's it been?'

'Mixed.'

'That's what I don't want. I want it made.'

'Change girls.'

'I want Jane. She spits on marriage, too.'

He had a problem. He asked my name. His was Johnny

Cass. I steered him on to the recent past of his career to date. This included the Peace Corps phase in Manila which hadn't given him the feeling that he had made much impact on the Philippinos, followed by free-lancing in refugee camps outside Kowloon, not convinced that he was contributing too much there, either. Jane, already tightening up for the next hop, this time to Mauritius, had been working as a secretary for an American bank in Hong Kong. She had parents in San Diego she hadn't seen for years. Johnny wondered whether Singapore just might appeal to her as a place to settle and asked whether I thought he could get hold of the Ford franchise there, which I didn't think was likely. It didn't look as though the Ford franchise anywhere was going to anchor Jane for long, she wanted plenty of love now but no backlash from it later in the form of little mouths helping to use up the world's diminishing food supply.

'On a bed we make it,' Johnny said. 'We really make it.'

She had come to Macao with him, from what I gathered, to round out another experience for her memory bank, filing these like case histories for instant reference in rare moments of insecurity, using them as evidence that she was really living. I was about to suggest that some human relationships, however satisfying in certain areas, just have to be written off as long-term investments but didn't get around to this for the public address system hissed into life.

'Señor Harreez, room two hundreds ten. If in hotel pliz come to desk. Señor Paul Harreez.'

'See you,' Johnny said as I got off the stool.

At the arch to the foyer I had a slight touch of dizziness, a fatigue symptom, but it passed quickly and I walked over tiles to identify myself. The night clerk had black hair greased to his scalp and, like the barman, had seen everything, but still found life entertaining. He ushered me past a lifted flap into a large room furnished for comfort all about a centred, tidy desk. The man who rose was mostly Portuguese but like so many Macanese had obviously escaped from his birth prison into the larger world, and for a considerable time, which rather made me wonder what had brought him back. His English was more than competent.

'Sorry to trouble you, Mr Harris, but it is perhaps important. Have you lost anything?'

'I don't think so.'

'You're sure?'

'You mean from my room? I haven't been upstairs for hours.'

'Not your room, your person.'

My hand went to the wallet pocket in my jacket. It was empty. I stood there feeling a fool. I had used loose change for my drinks and prior to that had been the victim of one of the oldest dodges in the world, if with a new variation.

'Is it your notecase?'

'Yes.'

He opened a drawer and produced a pigskin billfold. 'This?'

I nodded.

'How did you get it?'

'A girl brought it in. Only a few minutes ago. We tried to detain her but she ran away. She's not the sort that we . . . ah . . .' He thought better of what he had been going to say. 'By the way, my name is Ramirez da Silva. I'm the under-manager. Would you please check the money and other contents?'

I did that, carefully.

'It seems to be okay.'

'I'd like to be quite certain this isn't a police matter, Mr Harris. We pride ourselves on keeping petty crime under control in Macao. Of course, if you assure us that it wasn't anything like that . . .'

'What did the girl say?'

'That she found this after you had left her sampan.

She told my clerk that she had already received payment for . . . services rendered.'

Senor da Silva smiled pleasantly, with understanding, at the same time contriving to appear slightly shocked by my taste. I couldn't blame him.

'I don't want anything done about this.'

He understood that, too, very well.

'As you wish. And if you're quite certain there is nothing to report?'

'Nothing.'

'Very good, Mr Harris. May I say I think you were fortunate? One of the river girls . . .'

He shrugged.

'I'll be more careful in future.'

He smiled again.

'I might suggest that there is no great difficulty in arranging entertainment that might be more . . . ah . . . suitable.'

'Thank you, I'll keep that in mind.'

'Oh . . . there was a phone call from Singapore some time ago. You were asked to ring back. Here's the number.'

The digits said Ranya's apartment. The clerk was grinning as I passed the lifted flap. My stare straightened his face again. In the cage going up I had a sharp turn of dizziness and, though this passed by the time I got to my room, I was sweating. I sat down on the bed to make my call feeling very odd indeed and spent some of the ten minutes I had to wait with my eyes shut.

'Mrs Nivalahannanda.'

It was a good connection.

'Paul.'

'You must be having an early night. Or have you got a girl in your room with you already?'

'I left her on the esplanade. The better me won.'

Ranya didn't laugh.

'Is this line secure? I didn't try to ring you from the office.'

'I wouldn't assume too much. What is it?'

'I've found our leak,' she said.

'Who?'

'My secretary.'

'How did you do it?'

'Very simple. I talked about having lunch in a new restaurant I wanted to try, said I might be late. Twenty minutes later I came back to find her photographing the Bangka file. She had it spread out on my desk.'

Ranya's secretary had once been mine, a smooth, cool girl.

'What have you done about it?'

'Got a signed statement. This has been going on for nine months. She doesn't know who is behind it, she says. She was paid cash for micro film delivered. I always thought that girl dressed too well. I told you I wanted to replace her with a personal assistant.'

'All right, Ranya! You haven't gone to the police?'

'Not yet.'

'Don't. Have you sacked the girl?'

'No. After a big scene I put her on probation. She's coming in tomorrow. I thought you might want her to go on delivering film.'

'You're so right, I do. They mustn't know that we've cracked the Singapore end.'

'So things are happening with you?'

'Up to a point.'

She didn't ask questions.

'There's something else, Paul. A man called the office from Texas.'

'I don't know anyone in Texas.'

'His name is Ralph P. Brinkhausen.'

'It doesn't mean a thing.'

'He says he and you can do a quarter of a million dollars' worth of business.'

'What kind of business?'

'He's in oil.'

'I've cleared out of oil for good and nothing will get me back to it. What's his proposition?'

'He wouldn't tell me. It's confidential. And it has nothing to do with Hok Lin, apparently. One of your other businesses. I offered to put him on to your Kuala Lumpur office and that woman who runs it for you, but he wouldn't have this. It has to be you. He wants to know when he can fly out to see you. He's calling me back tomorrow. What do I say?'

'That you can't get in touch with me. I'll deal with this, whatever it is, when I get back to Singapore.'

'A quarter of a million dollars' worth of business sounds interesting.'

'It will wait.'

'Matters involving money of that kind often won't wait. However, it's your affair. Why don't you send me an airmail about what you're up to?'

'When I know more about it I will.'

'Good night, Paul.'

The dizziness had returned. I lay back on the bed for a while, then had to roll off it and make for the bathroom where I was very sick indeed.

I had a bad night. Food poisoning puts the whole point and purpose of your living in sharp perspective. It seemed likely that if I got what I deserved in the end I would die in a ninth-floor bedroom of a luxury hotel from which all the staff had walked out on strike and when you rang for help all you heard was a distant buzzing.

My phone hummed.

'Hallo, there. This is Amelia Jackson. How are you this lovely morning?'

What I said didn't actually become audible, which was just as well since she claimed to be an active Methodist.

'Mr Harris? Are you there?'

'Just.'

'What's the matter?'

So I told her, being astonishingly brave about it.

'Oh, my goodness me. These stomach things can be just terrible. Whatever were you eating?'

'Prawns at a night stall.'

'You mean a *Chinese* night stall? Whatever for?'

'I was hungry.'

'All I can say is you're crazy! But I always carry a small medical box with me . . .'

'Now wait, please, Miss Jackson . . .'

'No, I'm coming right around. What on earth are friends for if not to help when they can?'

She hung up. I got off the bed to unlock the door, then detoured via the bathroom on my way back to it. The mirror in there wasn't encouraging. Neither was water in both knees where there should have been bone joints. I had my head back on the pillow by the time Miss Jackson arrived. She took one look at me but didn't say she thought I was dying.

'Now tell me about it.'

'I've been streaming at every aperture.'

Her reaction was brisk.

'A good thing in itself.'

The medical box took up a lot of room in her suitcase. She produced a thermometer from it.

'Open your mouth.'

While I sucked she moved about tidying. I couldn't suggest that the hotel had maids. After five minutes she pulled out the instrument, shook it, and held it up.

'Just as I thought, you haven't a temperature. Were you sweating during the night?'

'I was doing everything.'

'You must have had a little crisis.'

She picked up the phone.

'This is room two hundred and ten. Mr Harris. We want a little beef tea and dried crackers. What? I don't know what you call it in Portuguese. The juice from boiled beef. *Good* beef.'

When the stuff finally arrived she spooned it into me. I had half a dry cracker as well and after that two pills. I didn't ask what they were. She then left me to have a little sleep.

When I woke I could not only sit up, my head had shrunk back to normal size. I got out of bed and went to the windows, taking great care of myself. The day lost must have been beautiful but now the Chinese mountains were darkening again. I had a bath and after it rang Miss Jackson.

She was in her room reading *War and Peace* for the fifth time. Whenever you went back to it you discovered new wonders. In the afternoon she had gone for a little walk and found the cutest little curiosity shop up a side street that just couldn't be a tourist trap. She had bought a little figurine for only seventy escudos which the man had insisted was jade though she knew it couldn't be at that price, only soapstone, but still terribly pretty, some kind of goddess with a sweet face. I could have a plate of scrambled eggs with a cup of tea and maybe something milky later on, the main thing to remember being that I mustn't burden my stomach, it was still in shock.

'Tomorrow morning after breakfast,' I said, 'we'll go to see that poet's cave.'

'Well, if you're all right again I'd love that. But you mustn't feel that you owe me anything, Mr Harris.'

'I don't.'

'You're making this a very happy vacation for me, do you know that? You get an early night now.'

'I will.'

From room service I ordered a minestrone followed by a fillet steak plain, medium rare, but when the tray came and I'd had one look I knew that Miss Jackson was right and I was wrong.

The phone rang. It was no surprise that the caller was Teng Ching Wok. There had been time for him to consult his employers.

'I must see you right away,' he said. 'Tonight.'

'Sorry, but I'm not coming up to your villa. Stomach upset. I'm staying in this area. Early bed. Make it tomorrow. I'll ring you.'

'No, Paul! This is important. I'll come to you.'

'I thought you never left your house?'

'I don't often. But I'm much better again.'

'I'm glad to hear that. How about meeting me in the bar downstairs? Nothing like the noise in the bar to give privacy.'

'I never go to public places!'

'So where do we make contact?'

'There's a little park at the end of the Praya. It's only a short walk from your hotel. Could you manage that?'

'Just. If I wasn't away too long.'

'You'll see a statue and there's a bench by it where we can sit.'

'You come escorted by your bodyguard?'

'No. I'll come in a taxi.'

'All right. What time?'

'Half past ten?'

'That's not too late. Sure.'

I hung up, pulled forward the tray, and chewed small pieces of steak to give me strength.

At half past nine I went downstairs to have one stomach-settling brandy in the bar, but decided not to try sitting on a stool, turning with my glass to find an empty booth.

'How about joining us, Mr Harris?'

It was a little surprising that Johnny Cass remembered me. There was one light in the booth, about five candle power and heavily shaded in a tube, this setting up a slight reflection from a black table top. I was introduced to Jane who, though mostly invisible, somehow at once felt formidable, a kind of emanation. I asked if they were staying in the hotel, but they weren't, just having a drink before they tried out our casino. When Jane leaned forward to pick up a glass I saw that she was wearing a granny dress, prim ruffles at neck and cuffs, which didn't prepare me at all for what was to come.

'Are you a crypto-fascist, Mr Harris?'

'Now, Janey!' Johnny said.

'I want to know, that's all.'

'It's not a label that's been pinned on me often.'

'But you're a business man in Singapore. Which means that you support the regime?'

'On the whole, yes.'

'I think that's horrible,' Jane said.

'Look, honey, let's not attack Mr Harris in the first two minutes. After all, I asked him to come and sit with us.'

'It's all right,' I said. 'I can look after myself. I understand you work in an American bank in Hong Kong, Miss Daly?'

'I have to eat wherever I go. The fact that I work there doesn't mean that I tolerate its ethic. And I'm resigning at the end of the month. Also, in that bank I've been able to organize a considerable amount of worker resistance.'

'You mean you've been coaching employees for strike action?'

'It's too soon for that. They're all too scared. The basic insecurity in Hong Kong is capitalism's biggest asset. All I can do is sow the seed. One day it'll germinate.'

'While you're in Mauritius doing more sowing?'

'I move about the world. I want to know the human situation everywhere.'

'It could be argued that you get to know it best by staying put somewhere.'

'That's not my view, Mr Harris.'

She didn't listen to any views that weren't hers. She might be as beautiful as Helen of Troy but this was no girl to settle with in an eight-roomed house in Dayton or anywhere else. Johnny's picture had given her soft edges, but he was fooling himself, Jane Daly was spiritual reinforced concrete to the extreme limits of her personality. I couldn't believe she was all that good in bed either. What Johnny was suffering from was that look-alike narcissism which sometimes happens, in her eyes he saw his own, in her mouth the shape of his, and unisex daywear helps maintain the fantasy. Last night in this bar he had seemed to have quite a positive identity of his own but this was now totally overlaid, all he could do was make little peeping noises of distress.

I sat there sipping my Courvoisier thinking about Ranya Nivalahannanda. She was a positive woman, too, positive about making money and setting up house with me, but if she couldn't have both she'd take the money. Hard she might be, she'd had a hard life only really made bearable by the glitter of her diamonds, but at the same time she wasn't a steam roller, she admitted that there were approaches to living other than her own and that these were probably essential in the general pattern. After all, too many people around as bright as she was would be bad for business. Sitting opposite Jane I was suddenly almost in love with Ranya who, out of the office, could be all woman for quite some time. To hell with unisex.

'If there is one thing worse than the rampant colonialism of Hong Kong,' Jane said, 'it's post-colonial dictatorship.'

'An inevitable phase in the emergence of a new nation.'

'*What?*'

'A new country must have order. And order demands discipline.'

'Oh, God! We're drinking with Hitler!'

'Janey! Listen, Mr Harris, she's just in this kind of mood tonight.'

'I'm not in any kind of mood, Johnny. I'm just as I always am whenever I run into raw reaction.'

'Are you a western Maoist, Miss Daly?'

'Janey's more like an anarchist.'

'Johnny, I will *not* have you speaking for me! What do you mean by a *western* Maoist?'

'Outside of China Maoism is a bogus Puritan ethic. Inside China it's a god cult. The two things bear no relation to each other.'

'I don't get that, Mr Harris?'

'Your western Maoist is all for those Chinese Puritan disciplines when he doesn't have to live under them. That's what I mean by bogus. In China Maoism isn't bogus because it's a religion. Those hymns the kiddies are still being taught about sticking bayonets into the bellies of the rotten imperialists may seem a bit rough for that age group but we have to remember they're part of a worship ritual. Worship of a god who moved to Peking in 1948.'

Jane put her glass down on the table. It was irritating not to be able to see her face.

'You know what I think?' she said. 'You ought to be preserved somehow like those specimens in a medical museum. You'd be *so* interesting to future generations.'

Johnny pushed himself to his feet.

'How about another drink all round? Was that a brandy you had, Mr Harris?'

'Thanks, but I can't wait. I have to meet a lapsed Maoist. Have a good time at the tables.'

Johnny wanted to come with me to the door of the bar as a gracious gesture but Jane wouldn't let him. Brandy, plus the adrenalin pumped into my blood stream, had made me feel almost normal and I walked in a relatively brisk way across the foyer and out into a night where moonlight was competing with sodium lamps and losing. I looked first at the mountains to see what their role was this evening, finding this the same, a brooding black. I went down the hotel steps past a pair of Madrassi youths strolling hand in hand and crossed over to the mole side of the Praya where light came second hand from the main pavement.

Beyond the sea wall, floating on a high tide, were nests of small sampans, each boat tied up to its own pole which had been shoved hard into a mud bottom. Transistors blared Mao music and there were shouted conversations. Farther out the anchored junks carried riding lights, these often eclipsed by the red glow from braziers on well decks, charcoal being fanned for a late cook up. The breeze was from the south, the one that keeps Macao cool while Hong Kong swelters behind its windbreak of high hills. Half-way to the horizon was a tight cluster of square sails, a fishing fleet bound for work.

Beyond anchored junks a small sampan seemed to be adrift, its stern oar shipped, no sign of anyone on board. It was moving as though powered by a hidden outboard and I watched for a moment or two before realizing that it was travelling on the current which sweeps past the city as part of the flow from the mouths of the huge Si-Kiang River. The South China coast has many of these streams contesting the ocean tides, refugees swimming to Hong Kong often drowned in one of them, but the most infamous is the Macao current. At times and in places this reaches seven to eight knots and an escapee from China who has misjudged tides sees the lights he was making for slide past while he is taken, only half anaesthetized by terror, straight out to sea. No one knows even approximately how many have been lost in these swims to reach Portuguese territory.

A man emerged from under the sampan's bow hood, making his leisurely way aft, picking up the long stern oar and fitting this into its wooden peg. He turned his boat with short flipping strokes that churned up water like a ship's propeller in reverse, but for all the effort it took him moments to get clear of the current into the light reflecting calm of the anchorage. He had been using that moving water belt beyond the harbour as a bird uses a thermal, not even having to steer.

The park was small, a triangle of trees and shrubs to mark the ending of the esplanade, the road past it narrowing at the swing away from the sea. The pavement followed the mole to become a cement footpath. There was a statue on a plinth, a European gentleman in bronze, the inscription shadowed away from any light, though it seemed likely that it was Dr Salazar gazing out over territory which, against considerable odds, he had been able to hold for Portugal. The place looked ideal for lovers but there didn't seem to be anyone using it. I saw our conference bench but went to stand by the sea wall.

None of the cars coming down the Praya slowed at the corner and their headlights, deflected by that turn, never probed the thick screen behind me. At this end of the esplanade there were no sampans at all, probably because a rock bottom resisted anchor poles. It was certainly a perfect spot for a meeting with a recluse, though I wasn't expecting him in person, just his deputy.

Teng's deputy made a very silent approach, announcing his arrival with the snout of a gun dug into the nape of my neck.

CHAPTER IV

Ho Tai and I travelled together in the sampan I had watched while it used a current. A mile off shore we used this again, our rower plying his oar for not much more than rudder control. My escort was up for'ard, squatting almost under the bow hood, that natural extension of his personality, a Colt, on the floorboards beside him. I sat on a cross piece half facing the boatman who was old, trained by years of deprivation never to notice anything he wasn't paid to. He didn't notice me.

There was no talk, the only sounds a lapping of breeze-roughened water against wooden planks and the creak of the oar in its pivot. Ho Tai sucked at cigarettes, lighting one from the stub of the other. He seemed to have stood up to exile much better than his master, no hint of a personality change at all. Once I had tried to pin the label of psychopath on him, but it wouldn't stick, he was in control of his own mind, not its victim. Every time he looked at me he was reminded of a failure and he hadn't developed a personal philosophy which allowed him to live with these.

Illuminations from the casino ship and the Praya were already beginning to fuse to form one glowing mass. Our speed was perhaps five knots and, as the effect of the current was broken up by deeper movements in the ocean, the old man had to work harder to keep this up, grunting from his effort. He was the one who broke silence.

'There it is!'

I turned my head to see a flecking of white at the horizon just to port of our prow, this growing almost fast enough to be a ball lobbed over water. The ball went on swelling, then broke like a halved peach to show the stone.

The bows of a speedboat were throwing up symmetrical curves of spray and, whatever was powering that craft, it wasn't a Harris diesel.

Vibration began to reach us through the sampan's planking. The launch was much bigger than I had thought at first, with a raised deck over a cabin for'ard, but the cockpit uncovered, as though to keep the boat's profile as low as possible. It was painted an all over grey which in hazed moonlight was good camouflage. Wipers were at work on the spray screen, flicks of brightness. About a quarter of a mile from us she cut engines, her bow waves dropping as if two valves had been turned off. Ho Tai tucked the Colt into the waistband of his trousers and then stood, letting shirt tails conceal the gun, as though he didn't want it known a persuader had been used to get me into the sampan. He waved an arm and a moment later engines rumbled alive again, the cruiser easing towards us.

I didn't say goodbye to Teng's deputy, just took the hands reaching down to help me up into a cockpit, landing on cork matting. The launch seemed to have a crew of three, all wearing black oilskins, the man at the wheel worried about his paintwork as the sampan bumped itself clear. Then on an opened throttle we went into a U-turn so sharp I had to bend down to hold on to a gunwale. Back in the sampan Ho Tai was still upright, his arms folded across his chest, balancing against the mini tidal wave we sent them. The skipper said politely in Cantonese:

'Please go below.'

I went down six steps into a cabin fitted like the interior of a workman's bus, twin rows of two place wooden seats facing for'ard. Beyond the top bulkhead was a john offering rudimentary equipment and with a pump handle for sea water flushing which the people in this accommodation before me hadn't bothered to use. When I came out of the place my queasiness had nothing to do with the movement or a recent stomach upset, though the ride was becoming uncomfortable enough, not so much a pitching as a series of teeth-jarring slaps that seemed likely to put serious strain even on a welded steel hull. Vibration passed tolerance level. I went back to the access hatch, found this locked, pounded on it, and when it opened told a sailor that I didn't travel shut up in a mobile latrine in which the stink would have overpowered a pig. My command of Cantonese at his level seemed to startle the man and he stood back, letting me up. I sat on a bench a couple of feet from the helmsman which put me well below the level of the spray screen so I had no view for'ard. I looked aft at China receding, Macao now only a faint pinkish glow.

In half an hour we were all of twenty miles from the coast, shore lights gone, only the last hump of a mountain hanging on as though refusing to be put down by the horizon. Then it disappeared, too, leaving nothing but our churned wake. I was feeling very cold and one of the sailors noticed this, for I was given a steamer rug. I went on shivering for perhaps another twenty minutes until rope fenders were put over our side, then stood to see, directly ahead, the black silhouette of a big ship.

I can identify most of the bigger vessels plying our seas regularly even from a night cutout profile, but I couldn't name this one. The nearer we got the bigger she became, between five and seven thousand tons gross at least, and a passenger carrier from the bulk and length of her centrecastle. She had a dumpy funnel of the kind convention still planks down on the boat deck of many new motor vessels but only one mast, this just aft of the bridge, a solid tower for radar scan and electronic devices. My guess put her not more than five years old, possibly newer. Her lines said she had been built for speed.

'What ship is that?' I shouted above the noise.

No one seemed to hear.

The blackness of a big hull had now faded to grey, the

naval colour, this unrelieved anywhere, even on funnel, upper decks or mast. It was a strange paint scheme for a ship with rakish lines but even stranger were no riding lights that I could see, and not the hint of a glimmer from porthole or deckhouse window. We were within a hundred yards of her side before I made out that a door not far above the water line was open, with a rope ladder dangling from it, but again that square was completely dark, and our fenders had bumped before a thin torch beam shone down on us. I had about ten feet to climb, a sailor below holding the ladder steady while I did it. A voice above said in English :

'Please watch step.'

'A better light would be useful,' I suggested.

'In one minute only.'

The torch beam guided me over cork matting and through a canvas shelter rigged like a tent behind the bulkhead door, standard blackout procedure. When a flap was lifted I was dazzled by brightness in a long passage on a utility deck, steel painted white with fat steam pipes overhead.

'This way please.'

I followed a man dressed in a Hong Kong business two piece whose ears supported hook-over spectacles. When he looked at me I saw a long face for a Chinese, with stress markings suggesting an accountant who lives with the thought that he may soon be declared redundant.

'What's the name of this ship?'

'My name Ping,' the accountant said. 'I am so sorry you have difficulties to come here.'

'That's all right, I'm quite used to travelling to business conferences at the point of a gun.'

He stopped dead.

'Gun?'

'Your Macao sub-agent had a Colt.'

Mr Ping seemed really disturbed.

'I not know this. Most unfortunate. Will you please come this way, Mr Harris.'

We reached a cross corridor and right in the middle of it was an elevator with its doors back, these showing a cage panelled in teak. We got in, my guide pressed a button and the doors closed.

'What's the name of this ship, Mr Ping?'

'Tomorrow all things explained, Mr Harris.'

'You mean you're not authorized to tell me anything tonight?'

'Perhaps.'

There was something wrong somewhere in Mr Ping's life patterns which could be the old problem of not being able to reconcile ambition with what had actually happened to him. Doors opened and we went out into a foyer decorated by someone who specialized in cinema entrance areas, brightness painful to the eyes. A port corridor leading from it had handrails for stormy weather and beautifully veneered cabin doors with names instead of numbers. We passed 'Gardenia', 'Convolvulus' and 'Yellow Iris'. It seemed I was in 'White Lotus'. Mr Ping stood back to let me step over the sill.

I rated top accommodation which is always reassuring, a very large stateroom with the panelling broken along almost the whole of one bulkhead to feature an indirectly lit and enormous painting on silk of a five times normal size adult lotus and a pretty big adolescent still at the bud stage, both sitting on green leaf rafts afloat on pale blue water. The lotus motif was continued with patches of embroidery on bedstead, curtains and furniture coverings. A door was open into a pale lemon-coloured bathroom in which the lights were on.

'For steward this bell press,' Mr Ping said. 'He brings all things.'

That sounded promising.

'You like whisky now, Mr Harris?'

E

I didn't have to ring for that, the stateroom had its own fitted bar with a really comprehensive selection of bottles. I was shown how to get at the ice cube compartment, Mr Ping keeping up a steady chatter designed to stave off questions. All I had learned so far about my host was that he had to be almost unthinkably rich.

'You hungry, Mr Harris?'

'I could eat a sandwich.'

'I arrange.'

He didn't use the bell, but took the excuse to escape. I stared at the bed. It was certainly inviting, no bunk tucked in against a bulkhead but free standing, flanked by twin alabaster reading lamps. On the pillow lay a pair of pyjamas which didn't carry on the lotus theme and in the bathroom was a Vanitory unit with a stool in front of it so you could sit brooding into an actor's mirror over youth lost, surrounded by electric razor and toothbrush, plus an assortment of other items to help fight the years, deodorants, talcums, night and anti-wrinkle creams, three after-shaving lotions and two male perfumes. There was more than I needed here to keep me looking presentable even under acute stress.

The thoughtful provision of so much in the bathroom made me wonder what there might be in the wardrobe where I found a Shantung silk dressing-gown, three pairs of Courtelle trousers in bright hues plus two jackets of the same material, one conservative, the other scarlet. Drawers held assorted underclothes, shirts plain and coloured, socks and two sweaters. I couldn't believe they had my shoe size too, almost relieved to find only a pair of slip-slops still in their plastic pack. Here was hospitality carried to its logical conclusion, you not only fed and wined your guests, you clothed them to your taste as well.

There was a knock on the door. My steward was young, personable, and had been trained to smile as he came into cabins. He was carrying a tray with a flask on it and there was a hump under a white napkin. He put his load on a table.

'What's your name?'

'Tsao Fu, Excellency.'

It is pleasing to be given ambassadorial rank.

'What's the name of the owner of this ship?'

'If there isn't enough here I can easily fetch anything you wish, Excellency.'

He bowed and withdrew, closing the door. A moment later I opened it. Tsao Fu was just going through an opening on the opposite side of the passage about three yards down. He turned his head, saw me, and bowed again.

The sandwiches turned out to be a personalized compliment, Scottish smoked salmon which is a food in a class by itself, totally different from anyone else's smoked salmon, particularly Canadian, which in my experience tends to taste like dyed whale, and I was sitting back chewing on the perfect solid to go with a malt when I noticed a writing desk with compartments for stationery and envelopes. These were all empty. It seemed a curious oversight in such splendidly equipped accommodation but when Tsao Fu came back I didn't ask about this, just requested some sleeping tablets, saying I couldn't find any in the bathroom.

It was an order he hadn't been expecting and as I hoped it would it took him far afield. Two minutes later there was no sign of him, or anyone, in the corridor and I had a quick look into what I had thought was a service pantry but turned out to be his cabin.

This was exactly what you get if you pay the bottom price for a luxury cruise to the Mediterranean on a liner with three lido decks and top-flight entertainers no one has ever heard of. It had a bunk, a washbasin and a locker. The air-conditioning vent gave out a smell of warmed engine oil, but most interesting was a special feature installed to keep a serf constantly reminded of his status, a row of six bulbs practically at face level on a bulkhead next to the pillow. If I woke up in 'White Lotus' at three in the morning wanting someone to pour me a glass of ice water I pressed a bell and not only did a buzzer at once scrape Tsao Fu's eardrums, but a light glared four inches off his nose to indicate which of the staterooms required a whim serviced. When I see arrangements like this I wonder why more servants aren't undercover revolutionaries, though perhaps a lot of them are, just waiting for the night of the long knives.

'Yellow Iris', which was unoccupied, was charming accommodation, too, also with a mural, and it had what 'White Lotus' didn't, printed stationery. I picked up a sheet to read:

'On board
MV *Hui Yang*'.

I was in bed with a copy of *Punch* thoughtfully provided by the management when Tsao Fu came back with my ration of two green and white pellets on a saucer, but I didn't take the sedative, just lay back in the dark thinking about the man who owned this ship. If he wasn't already one of the world's ten richest men it wouldn't be long before he joined that club. His name was K. K. Long and I had been watching his success story as a serial for years, trying to exclude envy as I did it.

It was classic rags to riches, with to me the irritant that he had started out doing what I am still doing, running tramps. In Long's case these ships were just a phase, step one, and he had gone on from them to step two, medium-sized carriers, and then to three, the real monsters. As an alleged penniless refugee from Shanghai he had somehow been able to scrape together the twenty-three thousand dollars needed to buy a twenty-seven-year-old coal-burning hulk and one of the tales going about had him outbidding shipbreakers by only ten dollars to get her. Certainly that ship had been put straight into service without anything like a refit, just the KKL letters slapped on over funnel rust. Two years later, trading with this tub, and on routes similar to mine with Hok Lin ships, he was able to buy another near wreck, and the year after that a third. Even allowing for crewing by Hong Kong sweated labour I wasn't able to begin to fathom how he had managed to do this, but his enterprise didn't just prosper, it snowballed, and he was soon acquiring the world's cast-off shipping at an almost manic rate.

What interested me, and a lot of other people, was the financing behind this. The Far East seethes with gossip about its successful capitalists, they are the big new thing, the general public following their activities with the devoted attention only actors rate these days in Western civilization, but when all the information about K. K. Long was thoroughly sieved not much fact remained. There wasn't a hint that Hong Kong banking was behind him, or Tokyo banking, or Taiwan interests, which island he had adopted as his official domicile. New York hadn't helped him, nor had London. There was no public issue in his company on any stock market. He seemed just to be a phenomenon of the times, an industrious Chinese with flair amounting to genius who in a matter of a few years was going to top Onassis plus the rest of the Greek shipowners in the amount of marine tonnage under the KKL flag. And while the other free port users have put checks recently on their building programmes Long has gone right ahead with his. I knew that he had two immense tankers as well as a hundred-and-fifty-thousand-ton bulk carrier building in Japanese yards, with plans for more of both types pending.

Long operates out of Kaohsiung in Taiwan, though his vessels are all registered in Panama or Liberia, whichever is the most convenient at the time of launching. This means that he avoids, like the Greeks, the great inconvenience of having to abide by international maritime agreements on pay and conditions. The key thing in shipping is to keep down overheads and Long certainly knew how to do this, working to his own standards in matters of crewing and maintenance.

He had the mystery man approach to tycoon status; before becoming big he avoided publicity and after making the heights became positively pathological about this. The Press never got near him, there were no photographs available, and if he had a wife and family they certainly didn't play with any jet set. He was said to be ascetic in his personal life, his one known indulgence this ship built for him in a Swedish yard and on which he was supposed to live for much of the time, which obviously meant that it was fitted out as an operations centre.

A mobile headquarters fully equipped with computers and data processing equipment isn't a bad idea in politically unstable South East Asia and Long, avowed supporter of Chiang Kai-shek and the free enterprise system, was in the happy position of being able, if the worst happened and Taiwan joined mainland China, just to walk down to the docks, board the *Hui Yang* and tell his boys to pull up the gangplank. He could then re-locate anywhere he chose, most of his real assets in the highly portable form of ships. Unlike me he didn't have to lie awake nights worrying about the future of the state to which he had committed his all, which could be one reason why he was doing so well.

If I had even been dozing I mightn't have heard the sound of electric derrick motors switched on up on the boat deck. This was only a distant rumble, but quite clearly from my side of the ship. I got out of bed without putting on a light, groping over to one of the porthole bays where a pull back of heavy curtains didn't allow in moonlight. Fingers told me that a steel storm shutter was helping to maintain the ship's blackout. By the time I had unscrewed the clamps securing this and yet another set on the oval glass beyond, the noise from above had stopped. I opened the porthole very carefully.

The night had stayed hazed and we were still at anchor. Down at that hole in the *Hui Yang*'s hull security seemed to have slackened off, there were lights shining from it as well as up from the grey cabin cruiser. The ferry had been away on another mission, this time returning with a full complement of passengers from the number of faces peering up from its cockpit. Their luggage was coming up first, handled by three sailors spaced out on the ladder, mostly bundles, but with the odd suitcase. Steel hawsers hung down from the boat deck to pick up the tender when she had unloaded.

While I watched there was an accident. The middle sailor fumbled a suitcase which dropped, hitting the tender's foredeck, bursting open and scattering contents over the water. The case's owner screamed in agony. This was followed by unfeeling laughter and after that a general Chinese din loud enough to waken anyone on this side of the ship. The thought that Tsao Fu might look in to see if I had been disturbed made me close the porthole carefully, then its shield, and get back into bed. About half an hour later the derrick motors were switched on, then the anchor chain came up and I lay feeling the gentle vibration from main engines on.

Daylight poured into 'White Lotus' from two unshuttered ports. There was the sound of sizeable seas smacking our hull but the *Hui Yang* resisted these from stabilizers out, her rolling moderate. Tsao Fu brought me a breakfast of kidneys and bacon, toast, freshly baked rolls and expensive English marmalade. He bustled about the cabin looking happy but contriving not to talk much. When I was alone

I picked up a white handset, dialled o and waited. There was a click and a voice in Cantonese asked me what I wanted.

'Hong Kong 376-4920,' I said.

'I'm sorry, ship to shore is not operating to Hong Kong.'

'How about Macao?'

'Macao is not available either.'

'Singapore?'

'No.'

'Then perhaps you could put me through to Mr Ping?'

A moment later I got a voice trying hard to be cheerful.

'Ah, Mr Harris, you have sleep good?'

'Perfectly, thank you. I'm calling to ask the time of my appointment this morning with Mr K. K. Long.'

A silence went on for so long I had to break it.

'Look, Mr Ping, I can accept the fact that arrangements for my meeting with Mr Long were unconventional to the point of damn near becoming a police matter. I can also accept his non-appearance last night to greet me. After all, the hour was late. But now I want a fixed appointment with your employer.'

Again the silence.

'Are you still there?'

'Yes. I am so sorry. It impossible you meet Mr Long.'

'Why?'

'He not on ship.'

'In that case why the hell am I on her?'

'All soon make clear, Mr Harris.'

'Mr Ping, I've just been trying to do some telephoning. No lines out were available.'

'Perhaps soon may be arranged. At moment not convenient.'

'It is not convenient for me to be cruising on board this ship however comfortable you may have made me. A great many people are going to be wondering soon what has happened to me.'

That was an exaggeration.

'Mr Harris, I'm so sorry!'

'Where is Mr Long? Am I being taken to Taiwan to meet him there?'

'I not sure where ship go.'

'Does your uncertainty extend to the Captain?'

'I not understand?'

'There must be someone on board the *Hui Yang* who knows where we're heading for?'

'Maybe no.'

'You mean you're all waiting for orders?'

'Maybe.'

I took a long deep breath.

'Do you know where Mr Long is?'

'No. But soon meeting is arranged.'

'Meanwhile I wait on this bloody ship?'

'Please do not excite!'

'Mr Ping, your employer may think he is a reincarnation of a Manchu emperor, but I don't! Further, if I want to I can slap a kidnapping charge on him.'

A wail came over the wire.

'All will be explain!'

I sat back against pillows the steward had arranged. It was one of those moments when a convert to no cigarettes longs for one. I tried to keep my voice down.

'Does Mr Long have a deputy on board?'

He thought about that.

'Yes.'

'His name?'

'Mr Percy Smith.'

That was a surprise. I haven't, as yet, heard of any Chinese Smiths.

'Is Mr Smith American or British?'

'No. Taiwan.'

'A Eurasian?'

'Yes.'

'I see. I'll talk to him. Thank you very much, Mr Ping.'

I hung up and stared at white lotus with offspring, noticing that in daylight the bud had a pink tinge. Then I got the operator again, asking for Mr Smith's stateroom, to be told that he was already at the office. I got the office and was informed that Mr Smith was in conference, would I call back later? After lunch might be a good time.

I kept my temper, a considerable achievement, showered, shaved, dressed and went up one deck by the stairs, having a look in the big lounge which was empty, then going out on the open promenade which was empty, too. Aft I found the major play area, Hong Kong wicker and cabana chairs scattered about a swimming-pool. A sailor was polishing brass. He looked at me, then back at his work. I went to the rail.

For a ship which didn't know where it was going the *Hui Yang* was travelling fast, from vibration and the track left on the sea this pushing somewhere near twenty-five knots. I checked sun against time, making our course almost due east which was the right direction for Taiwan. At this speed we ought to make Kaohsiung at the southern tip of the island by late evening which meant that if K. K. Long was waiting there I couldn't reasonably expect to have my meeting with him much before this time tomorrow. There was nothing I could do about this except cultivate patience, not a skill that comes naturally to me.

On a ship people who normally avoid all exercise find themselves going round and round the promenade deck under an almost irresistible compulsion, pounding those boards for a record number of revolutions, the fat panting, the lean determined. I did it, too, looking at the sea. No dolphin or flying fish were enlivening our morning, though a few gulls showed contempt for the *Hui Yang*'s speed by coming past her at fifty miles an hour, then slamming on air brakes to let the ship get ahead again while they lazily circled our wake looking for garbage. I broke the hike ritual by stopping in the glass enclosed area under the bridge to have a look for'ard. There was another solitary sailor doing some chipping preparatory to repainting down on the foredeck, not another soul. Yet if the passengers embarked after me last night were travelling third class, which I was pretty certain they would be, that deck below was their natural and only recreation area. The day was sunny, the hour pushing ten, and yet not one of those Chinese I had heard shrieking with laughter at a companion's misfortune had emerged to take the air.

I went up stairs to the boat deck and located the radio cabin. The door was unlocked but inside I found myself screened away from humming apparatus by ridged glass in which there was a small booking office hatch. This opened when I rapped but all I saw were hands and a white shirt front.

'I want to send a signal to Singapore.'

'No.'

The hatch shut. I knocked again but it didn't open. I tried lifting the thing myself but it had been snibbed. There isn't much use creating a scene with no audience so I went out on deck again and over to port. Here another door said in English and Mandarin: 'Gymnasium'. I went in, hit by a blare from a loudspeaker.

The music was at once familiar, a number from that longest running Chinese People's Opera, *The Sky is Red.* Unlike the President of the United States I've never actually had to sit through a performance, but that doesn't mean that I don't know most of the songs, for those of us who live in the Far East have had these pounded into consciousness in a way that not even a top Rodgers and Hammerstein piece ever achieved in the West. This item was the anti-imperialist march of the triumphant workers from Act Three. It is pretty noisy.

In the middle of the gymnasium floor stood a man

stripped to his trousers doing callisthenics. These were rhythmic and verged on ballet. He had his back to me and was balancing on one leg with the other elevated behind him to almost the level of my shoulder. Both his arms were extended and in use in what seemed to be a simulation of swimming. While I watched he changed from breast stroke to crawl. From this he progressed, still balancing on that leg, into an arm and body stretch down which wasn't a bad approximation of that poor swan feeling the first intimations of approaching death. I shut the door quietly behind me.

I knew what all this was about. Peking radio puts out frequent programmes of ancient Chinese body building for the faithful, these not only covering the motherland, but beamed to all Asia. It is a devotional item, really, via the physical you achieve the semi-mystical, one with a great mass of properly indoctrinated humanity who are also standing on one leg at the same time as you are, in paddy fields and offices, work canteens and the recreational areas of communes. Wherever you may be, even if solitary amidst the alien corn, you can get on that beam by balancing on one foot and going through the prescribed motions.

Mr Ping was very serious about what he was doing, and had been at it for some time, I could smell his sweat. It was interesting, too, that the music for the ritual was coming from a wall speaker, this indicating that it was being broadcast on the ship's intercom. I had the startling vision of a break for spiritual and physical refreshment taking place all over the *Hui Yang,* in the offices, galleys and crew's quarters, practically everyone, except perhaps the helmsman and that radio operator, at this moment up on one leg alongside desk, binnacle, and electric cook stove. If this was happening, and a total absence of people moving about suggested that it might be, then it was certainly strange that Mao morning worship was observed aboard a ship which travelled about as a positive symbol of successful free enterprise.

Mr Ping pivoted his body around towards me, this part of the drill. He had left his spectacles along with much of his clothing on a leather settee and though he was at once aware that someone had joined him he couldn't see who it was.

'I've always wanted to try that dance routine,' I said. 'Will you give me a lesson?'

The man's reaction was dramatic. He lurched towards the sofa, snatched up spectacles and garments in one swoop, then rushed past me to the door, opening this to disappear. I left the door open to clear the atmosphere, then looked for the knob which switched off the speaker. After that I mounted the electric horse, setting the lever to 'jog trot', sitting there being bounced, and with plenty to think about.

CHAPTER V

Though I couldn't get any messages out the security clamp down on a passenger seemed to have been at least partially lifted, for while he served me lunch in my cabin Tsao Fu was quite willing to answer some of my questions about life on board the *Hui Yang*. I started off by asking why I wasn't eating in the main dining-saloon. There wasn't a main dining-saloon, the officers had their own mess, the crew theirs, and the office staff one whole deck to themselves which included both their living and work areas, an arrangement that certainly spared them all the horrors of commuting. I gathered that the flower-rooms weren't often used and that, for all those lights near his nose when he slept, my steward had a pretty easy life. Mrs Long never travelled with her husband when he took to the water, and my subtle inquiries about other relatives, with special reference to a son and heir being trained to take over the business in due course, produced a complete blank from Tsao Fu which gave me the feeling that if there were Long sons they weren't in the company.

It might be that KKL was one of those too rare parents who had realized early on that he hadn't been able to breed top executive material. This happens often enough but only an exceptionally honest father can face up to the fact that his remarkable genes haven't been passed on to the next generation. It takes real courage to write off a son, buying him the subsidized farm suited to his limited talents instead of making him vice-president, and many a good business has been hustled towards insolvency because its top chair was kept in the family. In my view quite a case could be made out for this type of nepotism as a major contributing factor to Britain's long continuing near bankruptcy.

Had I been the eldest son I'm certain my grandfather would have had no qualms about giving me the big push, and not gently either, no rubber plantation offered as my portion. As Grandfather saw it I was a wild radical with ideas totally unsuited to the Far East, like workers' pension schemes, but the problem of keeping power from the wrong hands hadn't arisen in his lifetime because my elder brother was there being groomed for responsibility, a stalwart rugger forward who showed every sign of intending to stick firmly to Harris and Company's conservative traditions in labour relations and a lot of other things. The big upset to Grandfather's plans for the family firm's survival after he had gone had come when my brother died prematurely, as the result of a bullet, and overnight I was company chairman. I still sometimes feel haunted by Grandfather's shade, never an actual visitation, just an uncomfortable feeling that he is there and grimly disapproving of the way I'm running the business.

It may have been that still surviving streak of liberal

weakness which made me interested in the life patterns of the KKL office staff aboard the *Hui Yang*. I asked if these people were ever allowed to use those empty decks and public rooms up top. They were, but only at set times, in the morning before going to work, which meant very early since they were Chinese, and then again when they were finished for the day which was certain to be well after dark. Probably Grandfather would have approved of Long's highly individualistic interpretation of free enterprise democracy but, despite that label of crypto-fascist recently stuck on me, I didn't. It all seemed to smack too much of penal servitude.

Lunch had been on the light side which made my sleepiness after it odd. I've never been addicted to the siesta yet now that near king-size super-sprung mattress was almost irresistible, and though I sat for a time over a second cup of coffee fighting a deep desire to get up and fall on the thing, in the end I did just that. I don't think I slept at once, for I seemed to hear a whispering going on not far away, a hissing that swelled and faded, came up again, then went altogether. I went with it.

I woke with a fuzz in my mouth and a hammer at work at the back of my skull and before I even looked at my watch knew that I had been served a powerful sedative with one of my two courses, or the coffee. It was three minutes past five. When I stood I felt very dizzy indeed. Cleaning my teeth helped a little. There was a bell in the bathroom and I punched it. A moment later I heard a voice in the cabin, not very loud.

'You want something, Excellency?'

'Tea!'

I sounded like a colonial administrator of the eighteen-nineties yelling at his houseboy. The steward must have had a tray all ready somewhere for he brought it in while I was still buttoning on a clean shirt. He carefully didn't glance at me.

'Pour a cup,' I said, still the tyrant. 'Lemon.'

The hand holding the pot was shaking. He had some difficulty in getting my refreshment across the moving cabin floor to me.

'You'd like a sandwich or a cake, Excellency?'

I can't play the bully for long and this man was only Ping's stooge. Also, I had probably given them the idea of resorting to sedatives to keep me quiet.

'No cake,' I said. 'But open a porthole.'

He hurried to do this, letting in a strong breeze, then left the cabin with his head down, looking as miserable as the family labrador suddenly disgraced. I finished my tea, put on a jacket, and went out into the passage, conscious that I was under observation from behind that curtain drawn across the entrance to Tsao Fu's kennel. I took the elevator right up to the boat deck and went to a rail between derricks.

The *Hui Yang*'s bows were pointing straight towards a sinking sun. The ship was now travelling west, and quite as fast as she had been travelling east before I had my nap. I walked along behind the boats, all of these snug on their chocks, and tucked up beneath canvas covers, except the cabin cruiser which had brought me out from Macao. The deck under this craft was wet and there were still beads of water on a grey steel hull. The ferry boat had been lowered and in use while I slept.

The phone rang. I didn't think it was the outside world reaching me at last, and it wasn't, it was Ping.

'Mr Harris, do I disturb?'

'Not at all, no. I've had a most restful afternoon.'

He cleared his throat.

'I have message for you. Mr Long now arrives to Hong Kong soon.'

'Really? From where?'

'I not know. But surely he comes only to meet you.'

'I'm flattered. Many would think it was quite enough to have been loaned his yacht for a cruise. Is that why we've altered course?'

'Oh, yes.'

'So there's a chance Mr Long and I may meet to-morrow?'

'Oh, yes.'

'Good. Thank you for letting me know about this, Mr Ping.'

He cleared his throat again.

'You are interested in entertainments, perhaps?'

'Always. What are you offering?'

'This evening cinema show main lounge.'

'I'll look forward to that. What time?'

'Eight p.m.'

In the ship's tradition I dined alone with a half-bottle of claret that had travelled quite well. I went up a little before eight, hoping to see the audience assembling, but they were all already seated in the lounge which was blacked out, just Mr Ping waiting for me outside its doors. I insisted on staying at the back, claiming that to be too near the screen hurt my eyes, but actually hoping to gain a few impressions of the company gathered together from those first beams of light travelling over them. These, however, revealed high-backed chairs with only the tops of heads visible. Mr Long favoured short back and sides haircuts for his personnel.

The first screening was an old Disney short but no one seemed to find Mickey Mouse very entertaining. The KKL regulations permitted smoking during recreation and light rays had to pierce a thick blue cloud. I was rather isolated, empty chairs to right and left, Ping apparently somewhere down front on account of his myopia. In the brief interval before the main feature the lights in the house didn't come up.

Suddenly there was samisen music, a mournful twanging

F

which accompanied charactered subtitles set against a misty copulatory scene. It was a Japanese sex film that might well have been flown straight in by helicopter from Tokyo studios for this preview. There certainly hadn't been any censors at work on it. The *Hui Yang* obviously carried no women but in his beneficent way G. K. Long tried to compensate for this with regular doses of really detailed dream material. There was absolutely no need for any dubbing of the dialogue which for most of the time wasn't that at all, just noises.

In Kyoto I was once shown a celebrated, but hidden from public exhibition, *shunga* of Utamaro, a straight-forward erotic book which also had great artistic merit. The film made a bid for art, but failed, its story line extremely simple, about a samurai who wasn't so hot as a two-sword man, just a prodigious performer with the ladies. We stayed with the male lead but the ladies kept changing for variety. After about half an hour I got up, not from any upsurge of the puritanical in my blood lines, simple bore-dom, and was followed out into the foyer by a Ping who must have been keeping an eye on me and now looked worried.

'You not like, Mr Harris?'

'It's a very old plot,' I said.

He didn't seem to understand.

'After this travel in Switzerland.'

'I think I'll give Switzerland a miss tonight and go to bed. It looks as though I can expect a big day tomorrow.'

He watched me cross to the lift and as the door closed I lifted a hand in a signal of farewell.

Outside my cabin door I paused, remembering that well stocked bar, but decided I had seen too much of 'White Lotus' recently, continuing aft past Tsao Fu's curtain which had no light behind it, to a stair leading up to the veranda café. This area was only dimly lit, clearly out of bounds for off duty staff, and out on the open deck beyond the pool there were no lights of any kind. I went as far towards the stern as I could get at this level, pulled around a cabana chair, sitting to face our wake which was now marked by sketched-in lines of phosphorescence.

Vibration was moderate, the *Hui Yang*'s lift and fall gentle, our speed much reduced to perhaps fifteen knots or less. It seemed probable that the waiting to which I had been subjected was deliberate, part of the campaign against my interests that had started with the attack on Hok Lin Shipping, but if K. K. Long was expecting to find me suffering from nervous tension tomorrow he was going to be disappointed. I felt very relaxed indeed, and now that the after-effects of dope had worn off, much the better for that long rest. I was sure I would sleep well tonight, too. There was no point at this stage in trying to find the answers to a considerable heap of questions in my mind, so I just let them lie, lulled by the movement and a breeze that was brisk but had no chill. The moon was trying to defeat cloud haze but stars couldn't pierce this and with my back to the ship's layered decks I was in almost complete darkness.

From where our pleasantly illumined wake formed its widest V came a tiny flash, then another. I thought it was probably from a can thrown out with galley waste but when the glimmer came again, and in the same position, I had to rule that out. I wasn't at once alerted but the object back there kept on winking and I sat up. It was much too far astern to have anything to do with a towed mileometer and an object that could maintain our speed against the thrust of the *Hui Yang*'s propellers had to be powered. Then a disc catching diluted moonlight was suddenly elevated well above water. We were being followed by a submarine.

I lost that relaxed feeling. The South China Sea is certainly one of those areas which you expect to find secretly patrolled by underwater craft, this on account of big trouble on many of the shores fringing it, but these ships don't advertise, particularly if their engines are nuclear, and they certainly don't casually reveal themselves to passing surface vessels. I don't know why the idea of nuclear power came into my mind for we were nearing Hong Kong and it was perfectly possible that the British were holding a mini-exercise with conventionally powered submersibles, part of the game a mock tailing of a passing liner. Yet I felt a *frisson*, the one that comes to a lot of us at even the idea of anything nuclear suddenly near at hand. I stared at that disc, still elevated, and it seemed to be staring back at me.

The *Hui Yang* altered course, the curve in her wake noticeable. For a moment I thought the bridge had spotted the periscope, but there was no alarm klaxon, our lights stayed on and we didn't start zig-zagging or put on speed, so it could only have been a normal correction. The sub made that correction, too.

For half an hour I watched that rod with an eye at the end of it and was still doing this when it swung sharply to port and moved out of our wake, leaving behind its own pencil line of phosphorescence. The thing's spurt of speed was astonishing, it came after us like a sports car about to pass a lorry, then veered off, widening the distance from the *Hui Yang* until I lost it altogether.

A torch probed from up beyond the pool. A voice called :
'Mr Harris? You here?'
'Yes.'
'What you do?'
Ping sounded querulous.

I didn't sleep as well as I had expected to. A contributing factor to this could have been the idea of an outsize submarine equipped with long distance missiles nosing around us in the dark, but just before dawn it was something else, an intermittent thumping that I thought at first came from steam pipes concealed by my false ceiling. I listened to the noise for all of twenty minutes before realizing that it was from pounding feet, my bed directly under the promenade deck. If the office workers' recreation time on board the *Hui Yang* started before dawn this was something I had to see. I put on the silk robe and without even combing my hair went along to the lift, stepping out from this between two rubber plants and suddenly glad of the concealment these offered. The decks outside were brightly lit, unbroken blackness over the sea beyond them, and both the starboard and port doors from the foyer were fastened back. Passing each were men in office suitings, one or two even wearing hats, pairs, groups of three and the anti-social solitary. They were all making the circuit one way to avoid traffic confusion and walking pretty fast, as though the rules demanded this. Snatches of talk came in, though the pace was a bit fast for much of this, and but for that chat what I watched could have been the exercise period at Sing Sing.

I didn't much like the spectacle. Certainly I think disciplines are called for if a society is going to hang together, but discipline doesn't mean regimentation, which is probably why I don't go along with capitalistic paternalism on the Japanese model. This was the Chinese model and worse, much worse.

I stepped back into the cage and went up one deck, half expecting to find the ship's officers marching up and down behind the boats, but I had the place to myself except for one uniformed figure well above me out on a bridge wing. He stared down as though shocked by the sight of a man out in public with his feet in slip-slops. I flapped over to a rail between davits where I would be out of the officer's vision.

Dawn had just arrived and dead ahead was a lump of land. This took shape to become Mount Stenhouse, which is the first thing you see when approaching Hong Kong from the south, the centrepiece of one of the outlying islands included in that old lease to the British. There was a high cloud overhang which looked as though it would last to keep the day gloomy, probably the right backdrop to what was going to happen to me during it. Light was already firm when I noticed a speck to the right of the mountain, this swelling like a medical film's speed up of a growth on the grey skin of sky. The helicopter was big before I heard its clattering.

At the top of stairs I listened for marching feet below, but no sound came and I went down to find that the exercise period was over, taking up station behind a window with a view of the foredeck. The pilot had made this landing so often he had become casual about the operation and there was no preliminary circling, the hover lasting only for seconds, followed by a sudden express drop. She hit like an old bedstead thrown out of a third story, the undercarriage splaying. While rotor blades slowed sailors rushed a flight of steps up to the cabin door. This opened and almost at once out popped a short, plump man wearing a Harris tweed check suit that would have kept him really cosy in an Icelandic summer. In one hand he carried something I hadn't seen for years, a deerstalker, which he clapped on his head as soon as he felt the breeze blowing. Given one of those carved horn-handled staves he could have been a Chinese Scottish laird returning from the Inverness Highland Games, and though this might seem a big comedy act now I'm not so sure that it will twenty years from now. No one else emerged from the cabin, the pilot staying in the cockpit waiting to be lowered to the hangar.

I hurried down the promenade deck in the hope of accidentally bumping into my host in foyer or passages but saw no sign of him at all even though I loitered, so went to my cabin and ordered an early breakfast.

Hong Kong came in very loud and clear on the transistor set supplied at my request, with the news in English, but there didn't seem to be any excitement at all about the sudden disappearance from Macao of prominent Singapore business man, Paul Harris, international events swamped this morning by a local happening which didn't seem all that important to me. The police had detained for questioning the man suspected of being the head of the Russian espionage service in the colony who turned out to be a Chinese exporter of children's toys called Wang Kee Fatt. The announcer's voice held a scarcely disguised note of outrage that a Chinese should be doing this job for the Russians, though Moscow's choice for area supervisor seemed the logical one. Also, I couldn't get too worked up about the arrest of one spy in a city which must have at least three thousand professionals of all nationalities engaged in this business, plus something like an army corps of part time helpers. My interpretation of a news item was that it had suddenly been decided at Government House that the arrest of a Russian spy in the colony would do a lot towards further improving the already much improved relations with Peking. Moscow might be irritated by the move, but Russian trade is irrelevant to the economy of Hong Kong, whereas good relations with Mao's China are definitely the basic ingredient in the continuance of the status quo which is so desirable to British and other interests. If tomorrow's news mentioned Peking's satisfaction at the cleaning out of a nest of revisionist vipers then a little tactical exercise, with Mr Wang as the fall guy, could be rated a considerable success, possibly even resulting in three extra Hong Kong pavilions at the annual Canton Trade Fair.

I was sitting with this cynicism and a second cup of coffee when the phone burred.

'Mr Harris?'

'Yes.'

'This is Long Kao Kin at your service. At last.'

I was just a little surprised by this opening to our contact. You kidnap a man and then announce that you are at his service in the merry tones of a school playground's comedian. My riposte was rather formal.

'Now that you are on board, Mr Long, can I assume that the clamp down on lines of communication out is lifted? I'd like to phone Singapore right away. Perhaps you'll give ship's exchange their clearance?'

'I suggest we preserve security until we've had our discussion.'

'You mean I am still being held *incommunicado*?'

'I can understand your irritation, Mr Harris.'

'Irritation is too mild a word for it.'

'I know, I know. This whole matter has been most disgracefully mismanaged. I was shocked when I heard the details in my Hong Kong hotel last night.'

I took a deep breath, then said:

'You spent the night in Hong Kong?'

'Yes. I needed a sound sleep before I had the courage to face you. Particularly after what I was told. That you were seized in Macao and brought here by force . . . madness!'

'My word for it is criminal.'

'No wonder! That fool Teng Ching Wok! He panicked. The man has simply gone to pieces. Did you know that he lives in continual fear of assassination?'

'I didn't. It is some comfort to me to hear this.'

'Mr Harris, you will have my complete explanation when we meet. Shall we say in half an hour?'

I decided to wear the red Courtelle jacket, making my first appearance in Long's living looking like a marine warning buoy, but the owner's day cabin killed my sartorial effect stone dead. The décor was yellow, a loud bawl of the colour from fitted carpet to embrasure curtains, the furniture covering gilt brocade.

'Come in, Mr Harris, come in!'

My host had changed into a white shirt and white

trousers and he came at me like a large soft ball being bounced on asphalt. The fact that he was small and roundish didn't seem to worry him at all, life had given him so much else he could skip the beautiful physique. He took my hand and pumped it.

'I didn't know you were so big,' he said, looking up. 'We must both sit down quickly before I begin to feel over-powered.'

I was being sedated with a huge syringe full of good humour.

'This chair,' he said, patting it.

He spun himself around and jumped into his own seat. I half expected to see him tuck up his feet, but he didn't, these just reached to the floor.

'First, a most outsize apology. Will you accept it?'

'I haven't heard it yet.'

'My dear man, I am *so* ashamed.'

He didn't look it, just happy. For a Chinese tycoon his English was almost unbelievably fluent, a bit casual about tenses sometimes, but otherwise suggesting a great deal of use beyond the needs of commerce.

'I have come from England. Beautiful England. My runaway place. To which I escape. This time Ascot.'

It seemed to delight him that he had astonished me.

'Yes! The racing. I am there every year. But not, alas, in the Royal Enclosure. I only see the gracious Queen through my binoculars. Mr Harris, I am a Taiwan Nationalist Chinese but I will admit to you that my heart is in England.'

I took a moment or two off to try to get on a parallel compass bearing with this character, then said:

'For a man who is never seen and never photographed you certainly get about.'

'But of course! It's so easy. In England I am Pu Ching Kin, that funny little Chink fellow who owns pineapple plantations in Taiwan. I have two passports. Long Kao Kin never uses his, but Pu Kin is celebrated funny man at Ascot. And don't back the same horses as that Chink, chaps, he always loses. In England if you spend money no one asks questions. Mr Pu is a pineapple king who looks like his fruit. We all laugh. I am a success. Next year at Ascot maybe I am in the Royal Enclosure. To have the right Chink in your houseparty, that's rather fun, eh? A Taiwan Chink, of course, not a Mao Chink. But you must be waiting for my apology.'

I had quite forgotten about it. He became serious and this did something important to his face, eliminating the cherub, Long Kao Kin a much older man than Mr Pu.

'I needed to see you in complete privacy, Mr Harris. In such a way that no one, outside a few of my staff, knew that we had met. The complete mess which has been made of things is my fault, I should have handled this matter myself.'

'I forced the pace by suddenly appearing in Macao?'

'In a way, yes.'

'Is Teng your agent there?'

He nodded.

'In this matter. One uses a man of his type in such affairs.'

'By that you mean you used Teng to direct your price war, by OSL, against Hok Lin?'

'Yes.'

I couldn't complain that Long was playing the oblique Chinaman.

'You were out to destroy my company?'

'No. I was out to show you how vulnerable you are. You can tell a man this and he won't believe you, show him and he has to.'

'Mr Long, did you found OSL with the express purpose of using it against me?'

'That was only phase one of my plans for the new company. It is my hope that jointly we will be able to find an interesting role for OSL.'

'These are preliminary discussions leading to a take over by you of Hok Lin?'

'Not at all. I don't want to take you over. Quite the contrary, I want you to expand.'

'We'll come back to that, Mr Long. Did you know that OSL operations in Indonesia included the use of threats of violence to my customers?'

'This I only learned of recently. I must lay that, too, at Teng Ching Wok's door.'

'It seems to me that you're laying a great deal at his door.'

'Because I find it convenient to do so, you mean? Well, that's a reasonable conclusion, perhaps. The facts however are that a man situated as I am must delegate. In the OSL operation I had to have someone who could conduct the affair almost independently. I chose Teng. I was mistaken, but the fact remains he should have been all right. Look at his situation. The Chinese Communists no longer want to have anything to do with him. He failed in his role, they've cast him off. Mao's people have no sentimentality. But in Malaysia, quite aside from his undercover work, he was a successful and astute business man. Is that not so?'

'Yes.'

'So I took him on, giving him almost a free hand to do what he wanted. He has been a fool.'

'What are you doing about that?'

'Sacking him, of course.'

'It would be embarrassing for you if I pressed a kidnapping charge?'

'Very,' he said, then laughed.

'If you don't plan to take over my shipping company how do you mean to make use of me?'

He jumped up, back to bouncing, pressing a bell on his desk. It was answered almost instantly from an inner door, a man in glasses.

'Coffee,' he said. The door shut. 'Do you smoke?'

'Cigars. A box of Havanas was delivered to my cabin.'

'Good. What do you think of my chef?'

'I've eaten very well. '

'He's an Italian. But with French training. I pay him a fortune. When I am in Taiwan he comes ashore with me.'

'You have a house there?'

'Oh, yes, as Mr Long. Great high walls. No entertaining. No Press. The monk. Mr Pu escapes by the back door. I recommend dual identity to you. We are all natural schizophrenics. This is the solution.'

'You don't have another house in Taiwan as Mr Pu?'

'No, I don't. It's not an island for play, really. They are so solemn, the Nationalists. The Mao threat hangs over all living.'

There was the rattle of the anchor being dropped from the *Hui Yang*'s bows.

'Does this mean we're in British waters?' I asked.

'Yes. Off Lamma Island.'

'Does one of your identities have a house in Hong Kong?'

Long shook his head.

'No, I keep clear of the place. Too many rivals in the shipping business!'

Coffee arrived, brought by a steward from the door to the passage, the tray set down on the desk. Long sat in the chair there to pour, sloppy about the job, as though it was something else he usually delegated. However, he took the wet saucer, trotting over with my cup, then returned to the desk. He sipped, staring at me.

'I understand your Scottish shipyard is running at a loss?'

'Did you hear about that from Teng?'

'No. I was in Glasgow a week ago.'

'Not quite your Ascot England.'

'It isn't, you're right. That yard is hopeless.'

'The situation is serious but not hopeless.'

'Don't fool yourself, Harris. As things are now you won't be able to make it pay in twenty years.'

'And what have you discovered about my diesel factory?'

'The Japanese could kill it tomorrow, and may.'

'You recommend immediate liquidation on all my fronts while I still have some viable assets?'

He continued to look at me.

'You're a fighter, I think.'

'Thanks. And the K. K. Long organization has need for a fighter at executive level? Especially while you are being Mr Pu?'

He threw back his head and bellowed with laughter. I had never heard so much noise from so small a body. When he had sobered up he said:

'Well?'

'I'm not for sale.'

'I didn't think you would be. Look, Harris, do I call you Paul? I am Kin for both Long and Pu.'

'That seems a fair exchange.'

'I've been watching your career for some years.'

'Let me return the compliment.'

'And what did you find out about me?'

'Very little.'

'Good. Paul, I like your stance in these parts. The naturalized Oriental. That's clever, you know. Do they believe in Singapore that you have done this from your heart?'

'Not all of them.'

'Neither do I. But it's still a sound proposition for these days out here. You are as good a Malaysian as I am a Taiwanese.'

'Better. I haven't got a ship fitted up as a movable HQ.'

He liked that, too, celebrating it with chortles.

'Oh, we'll get on, we'll get on,' he announced, which

somehow made me more uneasy than anything he had said so far.

I was sitting with light from the ports on me while he had his back to it, so I moved my chair, noticing as I did that the *Hui Yang* had swung around on her chain and we now had Lamma Island about three miles to port of us. Long had produced a file from a drawer and was flipping through the contents which could have contained my dossier. I wasn't particularly curious about whether or not it did, more interested in the total dismissal of Pu whom I felt wasn't going to appear again for the rest of this top level conference, and he didn't.

'Paul, I could keep your Scottish shipyard busy for the foreseeable future and in a way that would make it pay.'

'Building what?'

'Coasters like the ones you've built there.'

'To use on my routes?'

'To expand the Hok Lin fleet for new routes.'

'This expansion capitalized by you?'

He nodded.

'Why would you resist that, if you had guaranteed management control? You floated a share issue in London to raise money.'

'From the general public. Not one man.'

'What does it matter where capital comes from so long as there is a massive injection of it?'

'A massive injection from one source means that source trying to run things.'

'No. I meant what I said about control left with you.'

'That's always the round one offer, Kin. It looks nice. But round two comes along soon after.'

'And what is that?'

'Interference from on high. It's like a law that comes into automatic operation. The end is the big shove for the original management. First an observer arrives from head office, charming fellow who only wants to have a look and has no official status in the subsidiary company. But he stays around, and gets the next board vacancy. After that there are staff changes at the lower levels. Then it isn't very long before the chairman is told that he has been under stress for years and that a world cruise is indicated to let him recover his health.'

Pu Kin would have laughed. Long Kin did not.

'There are alternatives to that assessment,' he said.

'Your money in my companies is going to mean some kind of centralized control. I like independence. I may be small, Kin, but my credit isn't bad. Bankers will back me when this is necessary. Singapore bankers. They know my ambitions have limits, that I want to go on running a family business. As such it won't ever become a threat to their much bigger interests. Also, I live in a place where people knew my father and my grandfather. That helps, especially with Chinese.'

Long Kin lit a cigarette, the first I had seen him use. He puffed out smoke and watched it drift upwards through the cabin's glitter.

'So your ambitions have limits, Paul? That wasn't the impression I got from what I have learned about you.'

'Dossiers really aren't very reliable. You can never assess your man properly until you've met him.'

'And when you do meet him you don't always accept his assessment of himself. It was my intention to provide you with the capitalization you need to become, and by your own efforts, one of the richest men in Singapore and one of the most powerful.'

He was staring at me. That round face looked as though it had never been cracked by a smile.

CHAPTER VI

A Trappist monk might have shown no interest at all
in this offer of top rating in the worldly success stakes, but
I couldn't. I listened while Long Kin set the whole thing
out on display, piece by piece. He wasn't really talking to
me at all, looking at the deck overhead most of the time,
his quiet, assured voice a form of gentle applause for his
own genius.

At first I thought the man who had once run tramps
was suffering from a nostalgia for the old days, that his
move from these to quarter of a million ton 'bottoms',
monstrous welded bathtubs with engines where the taps
ought to be, had left him somehow unsatisfied. But it
wasn't anything like that. He smelled real money still to be
made in the coasting trade provided this was organized on
a big enough scale. My scale with Hok Lin was comic,
bringing in a derisory nine to eleven per cent profit in
good years and next to nothing in bad.

Real success in our age demands two things, that you
never look back over your shoulder towards simpler times,
and that you always think big. Long's thoughts about
the tramp steamer business had turned up a vision of
a coastal fleet of seventy ships of from five to eight thousand
tons for the first phase and a mind boggling double that
number for phase two. This armada would operate
throughout Indonesia as I was doing with Hok Lin, but
from there push on up the coasts of Burma to India, then
around the vast peninsula to the Persian Gulf and from
there down the whole east coast of Africa. When I pointed
out that most of these areas were competitively served at
the moment the answer was one of his little price wars, this
to be allowed for in the initial financing of fifty million

pounds sterling. From the way he dropped that figure, serious but not trying to impress, I knew that he had it available, either in his savings account or from backers. The price war would start as soon as we could collect the ships needed to issue our challenge.

My Scottish shipyard fitted neatly into the picture. We could buy some of the vessels needed second hand but a great many would have to be built, the smaller ones keeping my yard's order book full for the foreseeable future. The yard would be modernized and automated for its specialization and costings could be regulated to keep the company's books in the black for the first time in its history since I had made the deplorable mistake of buying it.

Long wasn't in the least worried about our rivals' ability to fight effectively our bid to take over half the world for our specialization. As he saw it these companies were all public ones whose shareholders would begin to squeal when price-cutting reduced their dividends and to really howl when these ceased altogether. There is no doubt at all that a majority public holding is inhibiting to managerial enterprise, which was why Long Kin had never floated a single share, preferring to be elected chairman by one vote, his own. He had no doubts at all that within three years of our being able to cover the chosen routes with our ships the opposition would have fled, pressured by shareholders into accepting defeat, management forced to look for new areas in which to operate towards which, presumably, we would soon be chasing them. I could see that Long was already thinking about South America as a field for our expertise.

Those noises of shocked distress he had made about unauthorized dirty tactics used against Hok Lin in Indonesia didn't now seem to mean very much. If I elected to become a multi-millionaire under the auspices of KKL finance I couldn't afford to be queasy about the occasional use of strong arm methods. Of course I would be expected to pay lip service to commercial Queensberry rules but still be prepared to hit hard below the belt whenever I was certain a referee wouldn't catch me at it.

While that quiet voice went on issuing data from a memory bank I found myself wondering whether Long was the kind of man likely to train and keep close to him high level assistants competent enough to take over if he had a heart attack. The answer was a clear no, he didn't mean to have a heart attack. Mr Pu was his therapy against the threat of this, and when he felt himself beginning to twitch he simply nipped out the back door and flew to England for a while to play Pineapple.

Maybe he was capable of intuitive assessments of what his stooges were thinking for now he was staring at me.

'Well, Paul, how do you like the idea of the Harris houseflag flying on ships from Cape Town to Manila?'

'Beautiful. But don't you mean the Hok Lin houseflag?'

'No. Hok Lin will change its name to Harris and Company.'

'To give the general impression that the new expansion is European financed and managed?'

'Exactly.' He seemed pleased with his pupil. 'We will be operating in areas in which a Chinese company might be at some disadvantage. India, for instance.'

'There is to be no hint that Harris and Company is financed by KKL?'

'There must never be. That has been the whole point of the secrecy over this meeting. It is a secrecy we must maintain in future.'

'Look, Kin, both the City of London and Wall Street are going to be extremely interested in finding out where a small operator like me suddenly got fifty million sterling to play with.'

'Give it out that you have American backing.'

'Why American?'

'Plausible. They want to keep financial stakes in areas

they are leaving militarily. And American money looking for a good return certainly would never put a penny in their own merchant marine.'

He laughed.

'The kind of money you're talking about wouldn't be easy to sneak quietly out of the States. That's nearly a hundred and fifty million dollars.'

'Nothing for an oil company seeking diversification. As everyone is doing these days. The tobacco combines turning to breakfast foods.'

Again that laugh, clipped and under leashed control.

'You're diversifying yourself. Why?'

'Because KKL has reached a maximum for one man to handle.'

'You could always have another man at the centre?'

'I haven't found him yet.'

'Who is Percy Smith?'

'My personal assistant. He'll never be more than that. He's a Taiwanese Eurasian. His father ran a pineapple plantation. The one I bought. Are you wondering if I have plans to bring you in to the centre in due course?'

'I wouldn't come.'

'And I wouldn't want you to. You are Harris and Company.'

'Running a proxy business,' I said. 'Have you any more of them?'

'No.'

I wasn't sure I believed that.

'Am I on salary?'

'Fifteen per cent of the take on all new business. Until the first phase of our expansion is complete you take all the profits from the existing Hok Lin fleet. That is how you will become rich, Paul.'

For some reason I thought of Ranya becoming rich, too. It would appeal to her more than it did to me.

'You realize, Kin, that the senior vice-president of Harris

and Company is going to be a woman?'

'Yes.'

'You've had her vetted, too?'

'Yes.'

'I'd be fascinated to hear what conclusion you've come to?'

'Every now and then a woman emerges with a real talent for business. I think you have found one.'

'She thinks so, too. What happens, if, even with her help, I don't make it as the Far East's coaster king?'

He smiled.

'You wouldn't have any reason to complain about your golden handshake. Or your income for life. But that won't happen.'

'How about my diesel factory? You're not incorporating it?'

'No. But I may use my influence to see that the Japanese don't destroy it.'

'You look after your boys, don't you?'

'Yes. You have nothing to lose.'

'Just freedom.'

'You won't lose that. I've told you, no showering of directives from me. You have complete control.'

I wasn't too sure about that. We were sitting in a floating HQ which meant that Long could sail down to his proxy's home territory at any time, and no one any the wiser except the proxy. The *Hui Yang* would anchor over the horizon in the lee of some island and I would be taken out to her in a speedboat.

'I take it that the agreement between us will have to be something formal?'

'Of course. A contract.'

'Copy to me?'

'That would be unwise. For security reasons all records essential to our arrangement will be kept on this ship.

No duplicates anywhere else. You can see the sense of that?'

'I suppose so. How am I to be financed?'

'Through a Swiss bank in Tokyo.'

'What kind of communication between us?'

'Short wave radio between this ship and your house in Singapore. Not your office, I think. When we do have to be in touch we'll use a special code that is now being computer plotted.'

He sat back in his chair, quite ready for more questions if I had them. He wasn't even contemplating the possibility that I might turn down his proposition. I had been under observation for some time, subjected *in absentia* to a variety of litmus tests all of which had stayed the colour which said I was his man. Oddly, I didn't find this flattering.

The phone rang on the desk. I thought Long was going to snap that we weren't to be interrupted, but he listened, frowning. Then he said in Cantonese:

'We're in British waters. This is the only Far East base they have left. We can expect some activity from their navy.'

He put down the receiver.

'Trouble?' I asked.

'I shouldn't think so. Some naval vessels out there. The Captain thinks they're looking for something.'

I got up and went to one of the big portholes. There were three corvettes, grey, fast moving ships using helios for signalling as if they had a reason to keep radio silence. One of them went into an emergency stop while I watched, reversed screws turning up sea like an eggbeater.

'Is it so exciting?' Long asked from his chair.

'Quite. I think they're hunting a submarine.'

'As an exercise?'

'I'm not sure. I'd like to watch this from the deck.'

'Paul, this is surely scarcely the moment . . .'

'The sub could be Russian. We were followed in here last night. By a periscope. I kept it in sight for a while. Then it changed course and I lost it. But I estimate it was doing at least twenty-five knots.'

'That's fast for a submarine?'

'Submerged, yes. Unless it's atomic powered.'

It was a moment before he said :

'You think it was watching this ship?'

'It certainly seemed to be tailing us.'

'And you didn't report this?'

'I'm only a passenger.'

I walked across the cabin, opened the door, and went out. Long joined me at the lift doors, carrying binoculars. For a plump man he could move fast without showing any signs of breathlessness. We went up and then out on to the starboard promenade deck. All three corvettes were now almost motionless at about three miles from the *Hui Yang,* obviously listening on sonics. Long handed me the glasses and I made out activity on the stern deck of one of the ships.

'Have you some idea what this is all about?' he asked.

'You didn't listen to the morning news?'

'No.'

'They've detained a man in Hong Kong suspected of being the head of the Russian spy ring there.'

'So?'

'It looks like being made into quite a big thing. It's my guess this is a bid to improve relations with Peking. But the Russians have a reputation for never writing off spies who fail. First they try to salvage the network, then do something about the captured man himself.'

'What do you mean by that?'

'Well, they got one of their top men out of an English jail.'

'You think that submarine was coming in on a rescue mission?'

'Yes. To pick up the mice scattering from an uncovered nest.'

'Why should they want to tail us?'

'Wouldn't you be interested in a ship sailing on your rendezvous course when you were engaged in such a delicate mission?'

'I see. But it has nothing to do with us really.'

'Except that we've just anchored in British waters. And Lamma Island could have been the Russian rendezvous point. It's thinly populated. A good one. Easily reached by junk from Hong Kong. The British could have guessed that, too.'

'Just exactly what are you suggesting, Paul?'

'That there will be a naval boarding party to search this ship within the hour.'

Long stared at the corvettes for all of half a minute; then he asked:

'What's to stop us raising anchor and sailing?'

'At least one corvette.'

'You think they would put shots across our bows?'

'If you didn't stop on order, yes.'

'Then the situation is awkward.'

If this was a specimen of Long's reaction to acute crises I could see how he had got where he was.

One of the corvettes had started to move, swinging about in a turn which put her on a northerly course back towards Hong Kong Island. It began to travel very fast indeed, setting up a wake so frothed we didn't see the splash of the first depth charge going over, just heard the deep boom. A fountain of spray lifted and fell.

'They're serious,' Long announced.

'I hope not. I think that's just a warning to the sub to surface. The charge was a long way from target.'

'If the submarine doesn't come up will they aim for target?'

'I'd be very surprised if they did. I don't think anyone

really knows what might happen as the result of a direct hit on an atomic submarine that is probably equipped with a row of those missile ejection hatches along its back. I'd say that to date both sides have been at great pains to avoid finding out.'

'So this is just bluff? The submarine will sail away?'

'After a bit of tail tickling.'

'Very interesting,' Long said.

'It will be a lot more than interesting if there's a hothead in command of this squadron who decides not to pay attention to frantic signals from his HQ. The British turn out these types from time to time. There was that man Nelson.'

'The atomic age would have disciplined even him.'

I hoped Long was right. We were far too close to a potential incident that might conceivably trigger off World War Three, real trouble here giving us a zero chance of survival as eyewitnesses. And there was something markedly grim about this action even if it was only tail tickling. The corvette which had been dropping its charges while apparently *en route* back to a Hong Kong anchorage suddenly went into a U-turn, that would have done credit to a destroyer, to start closing again with target area, moving at a speed considerably in excess of its sister ships now travelling out to sea at about ten knots. I thought this meant the end of depth charging, but was wrong, three more went over in swift succession and seconds after the fountains I felt the shock reactions through my hands on the rail.

Tension had even reached Long. He had hung the binoculars by their cord around his neck and stood with his arms at his sides, looking oddly like an admiral grown plump over the years watching an exercise from his flagship. The drone of planes made him glance up, still wearing that expression of professional interest in these proceedings. His promotion to Chief of Staff might have depended on their outcome. There were three fighter bombers in formation which looked like Lightnings to me. Certainly they were subsonic and their jet trails plumed out behind as though they were Jove's cloud makers. From somewhere around thirty thousand feet they went into a steep dive which set up a vibrating whine against eardrums; the pull out, this with a terrible bellowing from engines, looking as if it came only a couple of hundred feet above the masts of the two tracker corvettes. It could have been a try-out for a bombing run. The solo corvette put over two more depth charges, these by my estimate well under half a mile from target which certainly meant that the submarine was really going to feel them.

The action was hotting up to climax or anti-climax, with me voting for the latter. The tracker corvettes were noticeably putting on speed, up from ten to fifteen, and then clearly – at least twenty, stretching the distance between them and us, which was something. There was no doubt at all that an uninvited visitor was leaving British waters, hurried on its way by those last kicks at its rudder fins. The ship assigned to depth charging kept up with the convoy and continued its work. Another underwater bomb erupted. As three planes roared directly over the *Hui Yang Long* turned to me with a shouted message.

'They must be very near the edge of the British zone. If you're right and they now turn their attention to us you mustn't be found on this ship. I'll order up the helicopter. It will take you to Macao.'

'Thanks. What's your machine's range?'

'Two-fifty. Plenty. Collect up anything in your cabin, the steward will do the rest. There's a door on your deck that leads directly out on to the helipad. Go along the continuation of your passage beyond the foyer.'

I went down alone in the lift. As I got out of the cage there were two more booms, muffled by the ship's hull, but still felt. The 'Lotus' room no longer seemed to offer an escape from reality. During the two minutes I was in there feet ran along the deck overhead and there was distant shouting. I hung the red jacket in the wardrobe, put on my own, checked pockets, then went out, leaving a tip for room service.

It was quite a walk for'ard to a door fitted with clamps for sealing in heavy weather. This was now open and I went through it practically on to the helipad on which the helicopter waited, the pilot already in the cockpit looking at me through an open window. The steps were pushed up to the cabin door, but I went to the rail for a quick look before boarding.

The Russians had not surfaced according to the international formula for this situation, the three corvettes about two thirds of the way to the horizon, and all bunched together, action patterns dissolved. They looked rather like grey cats who had just lost the rat. The planes were specks in the distant sky, but I didn't expect them to stay that. Our flight might well be made interesting by buzzing from a subsonic Lightning equipped to fire shells fitted with homing devices on their snouts.

The cabin had four seats for passengers and in one of them was K. K. Long settled comfortably.

'I thought you might be travelling with me,' I said.

'Shut the door.'

I did that, sat, and fastened my seat belt. The rotors started to scream. No one who does much travelling in these things has any need of mechanical exercisers, vibration massaged my whole body. The shuddering eased a little after we had swayed out sideways to clear the ship and half a minute later I had a good view of the *Hui Yang* lying beneath us, a sleek ship, built for more speed than any honest yacht needs. I leaned towards Long and yelled:

'Protecting the identity of Mr Pu, are you?'

He nodded.

'Macao has no airport. Where do we land?'

'Probably in Teng Ching Wok's garden.'

'What about the Portuguese police?'

'Teng can deal with them.'

Long didn't delegate authority, just problems.

We flew in quite close to the steep slopes of Mount Stenhouse on Lamma Island, presumably to make the helicopter less conspicuous, though I could see no sign of the planes. The corvettes had all turned towards home, their wakes making deep gashes on the sea as though they were applying speed as an analgesic for anger. With the end of British territorial waters now not far ahead of us I was beginning to relax when the pilot jerked his ear-phoned head back and up, seeing something I couldn't. His hands moved. We went straight down, an express lift contained in a tube, my body in the helicopter, my identity to follow later. Above rotor clatter came a high-pitched whistling like something heard in hurricanes, a great roar of violence concentrated into a whip for a strike. The cabin tilted. Beyond Long's head I saw a Lightning in a steep dive on course for us. It was like getting a glimpse of the shell that is going to blast you out of the world.

Noise was a physical pain. The plane must have pulled out of its dive just ahead of the helicopter, leaving us the blast of its jets. I was thrown against my belt, back on cushions, then hard against webbing again. Our drop was a death fall, uncontrolled spins with mind numbing vibration, din a crusher being dropped on scrap metal in a junk yard. The belt received and rejected me. Then I was suspended on it with the sea, seen through cockpit Perspex, like a rough textured blanket being lifted towards us.

I don't know how the pilot fought us out of that spin, I wasn't aware of him doing anything, but suddenly there was the sound of rotors again. The craft's nose came up, the sea disappeared, there was sky in front of us, un-marred even by a jet trail. I couldn't see the plane, I didn't look for it, just lay back on cushions as the cabin evened off. Long was doing the same, with his eyes shut, as though the way to recover composure, when you have lost it, is to keep still and allow it to seep back into your body again.

Perhaps a couple of minutes later I turned my head to see the bump of Lamma Island well behind which meant that we were clear of British territorial pursuit and unlikely to be molested again unless the Chinese sent up a couple of interceptors. Long had lit one of his rare cigarettes, as though this thought wasn't troubling him at all. My own thought then was that the pace for the contemporary business executive is far too hectic. In Shanghai where he had founded the family business my grandfather had taken a rickshaw to the office in the morning and one home at night. For exercise he played croquet and from his first drink at exactly six p.m. he never gave commerce another thought, concentrating on mah-jongg to which he and Grandmother were addicted. Every five years he took a slow P. & O. liner to England via Suez, the voyage using up six weeks, after which he spent two more in London before moving on to the Imperial Hotel, Torquay for the rest of his holiday. At the end of three months he got on another slow P. & O. for the voyage back east again. In spite of all this applied tranquillity he had made more money than I am ever likely to and in the process lived to be eighty-three.

The China coast was becoming obvious. From about a thousand feet up it really didn't look any more inviting than it did from sea level, but then an affinity for that territory, which should have been something in my genes, got left out of them. Whenever I've been in China the big thing all the time has been my exit date.

I stared at the back of the pilot's head which told me nothing except that the man was in perfect control of his machine again if he had ever actually lost this. It would be interesting to know where he had been trained and there was something decidedly military even about the way he sat in his chair, no suggestion of a civilian slouch, but with a back that could have had invisible bonds to a stake.

'Macao!' Long shouted, as though he thought I needed this reassurance. I looked out and there it was, Portugal's little outgrowth from mountains contriving even from this distance to look European in an archaic sense, period in a way that Hong Kong is not and never has been. I had the feeling that when high rise blocks took over from the coloured villas and colonnaded public buildings the place might suddenly lose its remarkable immunity, that suspended wave behind at last breaking.

I unlocked the safety belt and moved over beside Long.

'I think I should be able to pick out Teng's garden.'

He nodded, not greatly interested.

'It will be marked.'

'He's expecting us?'

There was a flash of Mr Pu.

'I certainly hope so. I've ordered lunch for two. Are you hungry?'

'I haven't been thinking about food.'

'I, too, was frightened,' he admitted. 'If such a thing was to happen on another flight I could complain.'

I saw his point, you couldn't really protest about a buzzing when you weren't officially on the aircraft. Long was certainly highly skilled in the art of never being where one might reasonably expect him to be, this an important contributory factor to his success. To achieve almost total invisibility in the world beyond your own enterprises, and to do this without inhibiting life patterns by playing the recluse, takes subtle planning.

We came over the little city by the back way, circling at sea to avoid flying above the harbour and the Praya, discreet in so far as you can be in one of these clattering contraptions. The pilot seemed at once to make for the right hill and I peered down trying to locate Teng's swimming-pool. Quite a few places up in the rich man's suburb had these, all of them putting up a dazzling glitter under sunshine favouring Macao. Then I spotted a cross made by folded coloured sheets, this on an unmistakably wide terrace, but was surprised by the size of the house itself; the roofs of the Villa Setubal weren't much more than would be needed to cover a middle-income bungalow.

The pilot picked out that cross for himself and we started to go down. I was about to shout that there was a fountain in the middle of the terrace when I saw he wasn't aiming for those sheets, but down beyond the pool where there was a small area of almost circular lawn. One always forgets how little space these craft need to land on and any old piece of grass will do provided you don't mind having the perennial beds all around it wrecked for the season by rotor blast. Here were no flowers, just a stout hedge.

A man came out on the terrace and stood looking up at us, wearing white, and shading eyes. He was too slim to be Teng. He walked rather slowly to steps and down them while we settled on spongy turf as gently as astronauts on moon dust. The rotors cut and the trees slowed their wild protest. I slid open the cabin door and looked down at a man who was scarcely bothering to play his part as a servant, bored with it. I jumped, still a bit weak at the knees as the result of a recent traumatic experience but managing to land on my feet instead of all fours. Long in his turn, however, lost balance and toppled over, for seconds looking a bit like a fat puppy wanting to play. He scrambled up, fury at a loss of dignity startling, a chubby face so contorted that my recollections of Mr Pu were suddenly overprinted.

'You *fool*!' He shouted at Ho Tai. 'Why didn't you get some kind of box for us to use, eh? Eh?'

'Sorry, sir.'

'Is that all you can say? Pick up my briefcase! Where's your master? Why isn't he down here?'

'These days he can't walk far, sir.'

'Can't he? Where did he find you? In a Macao gutter?'

I tried to be helpful.

'Teng brought Ho Tai from Malaysia,' I said. 'He was also a Communist operative down there.'

'Was he?' Long stomped up on to the pool surround. 'I'd have left him to rot in jail.'

When the great man's urbanity slipped it fell right down to his ankles. I followed Long down the paving and Ho Tai came behind us, carrying the briefcase. The pilot stayed in his machine.

Our processional had almost reached dressing-rooms built in against the front wall of the terrace when a figure appeared behind the balustrade above us, large enough to be conspicuous at once. Long stopped to stare up.

'And there's another fool!' he shouted.

Teng Ching Wok stepped back as though he had been slapped across the face.

CHAPTER VII

Long started off again towards the steps and what promised to be a somewhat noisy meeting with a business associate. It was just possible that the scene was going to be staged expressly for me, so I decided to skip it, stopping to look at the pool, tempting in midday heat. Ho Tai came trekking past me, head down. I went into changing-rooms which offered musty smelling towels in a cupboard and some gents' G-strings hanging on pegs. I stripped, had a shower, then went out into the sun again wearing a male bikini, having quite a long walk towards the deep end with its diving-board.

Up in the helicopter cockpit the pilot was chewing on a chicken leg. That red alert on the *Hui Yang* had still left him time to run through the galley and snatch up some lunch, experience having taught him that his boss rarely thought about food for the chauffeur. I bounced the board, then left it. The water was cool and only faintly flavoured with chlorine. I went into my crawl which hasn't yet broken any records, but was floating on my back when Long's voice reached me.

'Enjoying yourself?'

He sounded like a chairman who doesn't approve of staff playing in company time.

'Yes. Why not join me?'

'Lunch is ready.'

This was served alfresco on the terrace and I came to it feeling healthy. Teng looked as though he never would again. A bitterness that wasn't only from his ailments was gouged into that sagging face and he was making no attempt at all to be host. It was Long who said:

'Help yourself.'

I was doing this when there was a crash from the living-room. Teng jerked around in his chair.

'What's going on in there?'

'I dropped glasses,' Ho Tai called.

'What are you doing with glasses? Why isn't the girl serving?'

The voice that reached us was surly.

'She's burned her hand.'

I was in a chair with a plate on my knees when Ho Tai appeared carrying a bottle of rosé and more glasses on a tray. He looked like a butler who is only able to hold down his job because of the acute servant shortage. He left us to do our own pouring.

Whatever had passed between Long and Teng had exhausted all potential of small talk between them and I wasn't going to be the one to break a restful silence. Teng played with his food as though he didn't find the cuisine in his own house up to much, which it wasn't, but Long went back for seconds, a man with two identities to feed, heaping slabs of cold meat on his plate and digging into more of a heat-fatigued salad too liberally dressed from a bottle. There was no coffee, Long and I finished the rosé between us, after which he lit a cigarette and I smoked one of the three Havanas snatched in haste from the 'White Lotus' cabin.

That terrace was certainly an ideal spot, flower-decked, the fountain tinkling, the view giving it the feel of a sage's eyrie where a man could sit contemplating the world without having to become involved in its basic roughness. Teng, however, had not been able to make philosophy the cushion to his exile, and from the way he stared balefully out over Macao it might have been the outlook from Alcatraz back in those days before the Rock became Indian territory.

Long crumpled up his paper napkin, put it on his plate, then lowered the plate to paving. He stood, with his attaché case, looking down at Teng.

'What room can we use?'

'Why not in there? You can shut the doors to the terrace and switch on air-conditioning.'

'Which would let your man take a tape of our talk. Thank you, no. We'll use a couple of chairs by the pool.'

I was certainly being given an interesting demonstration of how Long treated the people who had signed on his team, and with no reason to believe that I would rate special consideration as the KKL proxy down in Singapore. The helicopter could probably land on my roof. When Long bought you that was that, and it didn't look as though I was ever going to meet Mr Pu again. Pineapple didn't play with his staff, only the kind of people who might one day get him into the Royal Enclosure at Ascot.

'Ready, Paul?'

I looked up but didn't move.

'For what?'

'To finish our discussion and let you read the contract.

H

I've got it with me.'

He tapped the briefcase.

'I think we've discussed your project as much as we need to and I can read the contract here. After I have maybe Teng Ching Wok can give me some idea of what it's like to work for your organization.'

Our lax host might then have taken the first jolt from shock therapy in a psychiatric clinic. His huge body seemed to lift from the chair, subsiding back into it again with much creaking of wicker. Teng stared at me and into that look came something I had never expected to see in his eyes, gratitude made shiny by a hint of rheumy tears. I had thought him long past any capability of love for his fellow men but for about five seconds he loved me.

Long was standing looking like an effigy of himself in ready mix cement. I had thought I had seen him angry after that fall out of a helicopter, but that was just irritation, this was anger. When he did speak his voice was pitched much higher than I had heard it.

'We will *not* stay here.'

'In that case, Kin, I think maybe I'll skip reading that contract today. I've a pretty good idea what's in it anyway. And I'd like to get this whole thing in perspective before I come to any decision.'

'While *I* wait?'

'Is there any rush?'

'I want the matter settled!'

'So do I, naturally. I just want a day or two in a hotel room by myself to look at every aspect of this project. Isn't that reasonable? After all, this is the end of Harris and Company as an independent.'

'I refuse to discuss this any further until we're alone!'

'Well, then let's make that discussion a couple of days from now in the Mandarin Hotel in Hong Kong. I'll book in there so you can get in touch with me from your yacht to fix up a time. Look after yourself, Teng. Thanks for the lunch.'

I nodded to Long as I walked past him, expecting to hear him shout, but there was a dead silence behind as I crossed the terrace and went down the steps. From them I saw that the pilot was up on the roof of his machine and seemed to be oiling the base unit of the rotors. They probably needed this after the stress they had been under. It was my feeling that Long would be taking off again just as soon as he heard his yacht had been cleared by the Navy.

At the barred gate I stood for half a minute wondering if it was going to open, but it did, with a click, letting me pass out into the lane a free man. I knew that I was more at risk now than I had ever been on board the *Hui Yang*.

At the siesta hour the suburban streets of Macao were almost empty and even the shopping area thinly peopled, as though most of the Chinese packed into this little enclave had caught a Mediterranean habit and went to bed after lunch. The shops were open but you couldn't feel that their owners were serious about doing any business until it got cooler and there was practically no wheeled traffic, all the cars parked along narrow pavements with windows down and unlocked, there being no trade at all in stolen jobs with China.

Johnny Cass sat deepening his sunburn in a convertible with its hood down. He had his hands on the wheel and was staring through the windscreen, but with vision turned in on himself, his beautiful face marred by disgust at what he saw.

I stopped.

'Don't tell me you've picked up the Ford agency here?'

He turned his head at once but it took a moment for vision to re-focus.

'Oh, hallo, Mr Harris. I thought you'd left this town?'

'No, I've just been out of the picture for a couple of days.'

He remembered our last meeting.

'Sorry about Janey that night. When she gets going that way it's like listening to a tape of a happy holiday in Italy.'

'Do people tape their holidays?'

'Don't tell me you've missed it? Sure. It goes with the home movies. Daddy saying just how he felt when he looked at the leaning tower of Pisa. Then you see Daddy looking at that tower. Maybe he says his feet hurt. It's a real spiritual experience. It's about what I get from Janey when she's doing her thing and I can't reach the switch off. Want me to take you some place? Anywhere in this town is twenty minutes. Complete tour one hour.'

I got in beside him.

'Did you rent this thing?'

'Yes.'

'Why?'

'I guess I don't feel human without one. Janey says I'm mentally just a projection of the automobile. I know what she means. There's a lot in it. I can see myself twenty years from now reacting on tape to the Grand Canal in Venice. And Mrs Cass will be right there taking pictures of me doing it.'

'Can you see Mrs Cass, too?'

'Oh, sure. We met first time when I took over her pa's new station wagon.'

'Sounds as if you're on the cure from Jane?'

'You're wrong, man. I can't get it started. Where do you want to go?'

'I was on the way to the hotel.'

'Still checked in there?'

'I'm carrying my room key, though I haven't used it for a couple of nights.'

'The woman you've been laying that good you didn't even go back for a clean shirt?'

I laughed.

'You never know, do you?' Johnny said. 'Janey and me walking around like a couple of sex symbols while a guy like you really gets down to it. And no recess.'

He started up the engine. We pulled out from the kerb and did a U-turn completely unchallenged by other traffic or the law. As we came down on to the Praya Johnny said:

'This thing has a gear change that's been operated by apes. Listen to that.' Then, running along by the sea he added: 'You come to a town and you memorize it. Why? Other towns get erased but not that one. Happen to you?'

'Yes.'

'What's the reason?'

'You walked with your love in it for the last time.'

He swore and braked hard for a swerving bicycle. Then he swung the car across the avenue and drew up by the steps of the Algarve, switching off, sitting with his hands on the wheel again.

'That hit me in the guts,' he said.

I could have just got out, but I didn't.

'Johnny, where do you go after Macao?'

'I haven't been thinking about it. Kowloon again, I guess.'

'Who do you work for there?'

'Nobody. I freelance. It's no place to be on a payroll if you don't need it.'

I knew what he meant. I had seen those refugee camps.

'You must have run into Father John Pelham over there?'

'Who hasn't?'

'You haven't been helping him?'

'Not exactly. Like I said, I'm not tied.'

'I met him once. Remarkable man.'

'Sure.'

'When there's no food for his refugees he gets down on his knees to tell the Lord that it's over to Him now, the camp staff have done their damnedest. And that night a supermarket manager sends in a load of dried milk and canned beans.'

'That's him all right,' Johnny said.

'He's the only man I ever met with a hot line to the Almighty.'

'I guess you could call it that.'

I opened the car door, then said :

'I gave him some money and he gave me his blessing. I went away feeling ashamed.'

'Of what?'

'I suppose it was not being able to keep my living simple. Thanks for the ride.'

There was no sound of a car engine starting as I went up the steps. The hotel foyer was somnolent, no one sitting or moving about, the desk clerk asleep on his feet. I went over to him.

'Are there any letters or messages for Paul Harris? Room two hundred and ten. Also, were there any phone calls?'

'Two hundred tens,' he said, swinging around to the mail rack. Then he added : 'Oh . . .!'

'What's the matter?'

'Nothing, sir. Please just wait a minute. I find out. . . .'

He nipped through a door into a room I had been in, closing it behind him. About half a minute later Ramirez da Silva came out. He had been having a nap, too, and was wearing a red silk dressing-gown.

'Sorry to bother you,' I said. 'I only wanted my mail.'

'Please come into my office, Mr Harris.'

He sounded like a bank vice-president to a client with a three-year-heavy overdraft. It is not a tone I like having used to me, but I followed him. I wasn't offered a seat.

'Now, Mr Harris, I must tell you, your room has another occupant.'

'In that case you owe me quite an explanation.'

'It might be that you owe us one!'

'You mean on account of my few days' absence? I'm sorry if that upset you. Of course you'd be worried about where I was. Did you go to the police?'

'We were not in the least worried about where you were and we did *not* go to the police.'

'Part of your service might be more care for the welfare of your guests.'

'I don't want advice from you on how to look after our guests!'

He was really hostile.

'What have you done with my things?'

'They are all down here waiting for you.'

'You mean I'm being thrown out?'

'You are being told that no room is available for your use and also that if you are seen in the bars or restaurant or casino you will be escorted out of them.'

'This is strong stuff, señor. I think I'm entitled to an explanation?'

'You astonish me, Mr Harris. It ought to be obvious even to a man like you that in an establishment of this kind we have standards to maintain.'

'And how have I ruptured your standards by simply staying away for a few days?'

'You really want to discuss this matter?'

'Yes.'

'Very well. This is a holiday city and we expect our guests to come here for relaxation. We are, I think, most understanding. At the same time there are limits to this. And allowing a sampan woman free run of our hotel is going beyond those limits.'

Señor Ramirez was not just being holy, he was very much a man of the world whose limited values had somehow been violently outraged.

'What did this sampan woman do?'

'She hasn't told you?'

'Actually, no.'

'Very well, I will.'

He wanted to, a lot.

'Some nights ago the woman in question was found in your room by a maid. The maid notified me. I went up. The woman refused to leave. She said she was waiting for you there, on your instructions. She had the impudence to tell me, in gutter language if I may say so, that if double occupancy had to be paid for you would pay for it.'

'You didn't make this a police matter?'

'Certainly not. The woman was ejected by three of my staff and via the service elevator. She made a great commotion in the process. Guests opened their doors. There has never been such a scene in this hotel. Never! The woman kept shouting that if she was put out she would see that you didn't come back here. It was my fervent wish, Mr Harris, that you would not. I have had your things ready since then to send to any address you phoned in.'

'It didn't strike you as odd that you didn't hear from me?'

'No. Your private life is no concern of mine. But you will remember that I had already suggested that a sampan woman was no proper associate for a guest in this hotel.'

'You mean you have a ten-per-cent cut on room service from the better brothels?'

Probably I shouldn't have said that, but I was in mild shock. The last thing I ever expected to have happen to me was to be thrown out of a Portuguese hotel in Macao for moral turpitude. Señor da Silva was staring, pop-eyed. He said two explosive words.

'Get out!'

There seemed no point in arguing; I wouldn't be happy here any more.

'Where are my things?'

'There!' he said, pointing to a corner.

And there they were, neatly packed suitcases with the attaché case on top. This had been in a locked drawer which shows you just can't trust hotels. I took the room key out of my pocket and the key to that drawer, putting them both on a table.

I went over to the corner, picked up my attaché case to find the passport inside. I checked this just to make sure they hadn't steamed off my picture.

'Have you made out my bill?'

'There is no bill!'

He might have been waiting for years to chuck someone out like this but I had at least got something for nothing in a gambling town which is more than most do.

'If you'll get a porter for this stuff . . .'

'You'll carry it yourself!'

'I think you're being unnecessarily unpleasant.'

'I don't.'

I tucked the attaché case under my arm and picked up the two bags. Passing the desk I said:

'What about my mail?'

'None, sir.'

'No phone calls either?'

'No, sir.'

Ramirez was in the frame of the doorway behind me. I looked at him.

'I could complain to the board for the promotion of tourism.'

'Please do, Mr Harris.'

'How about recommending a nice boarding-house?'

'I would recommend you to no place in Macao. I suggest the evening boat to Hong Kong.'

Da Silva was really enjoying indignation, there had probably been few moments in his life when he had found himself in a position to castigate the unrighteous. I might even have provided the first opportunity for many

years and certainly in that doorway he looked more like
the chairman of the local watch committee than a hotel
manager. I wanted to laugh but this would have diminished
the man's pleasure.

Outside the sunshine was still bright. The mountains
of China were still there and so was a Ford convertible in
which sat a young man staring through the windscreen. I
went down.

'Is your taxi service still operating?'

He came back from a trip.

'What? Hey, what's happened?'

'I'm an adult delinquent. Can I put my bags in the
back?'

'Sure. That hotel chucked you out?'

'Exactly.'

'What for?'

'Consorting with a lady one grade lower than the permitted level.'

'You . . .?'

He began to laugh. I had lost the impulse to do this and
didn't join him. I stowed my gear in the back and got in
the front.

'The problem is where do I sleep? The manager is
going to phone around to the other hotels. And probably the
better boarding-houses. A clean bed is all I can hope for.'

Johnny looked thoughtful.

'I might get you in where we are.'

'Where's that?'

'It's called the Castello Blanco. Cheap. Janey found
it.'

'I've always hated bugs.'

'It's not that kind of cheap. And it's got a bathroom.'

'Your girl may not like my sharing her discovery.'

'She probably won't even know you're there. You don't
see the other people staying. The front door's always open
and upstairs the passages go off like tentacles from the

landing with the bathroom. I heard someone taking a bath
once but that's the nearest I've come to direct contact.
There's no food. Breakfast at a café.'

'Clean?'

'The sheets are. Maybe not much else.'

'Take me to it.'

We drove into the old quarter, up a cobbled street, and
Johnny Cass had to tuck the convertible right into a
gutter to keep it from blocking traffic. There was no sign,
just a door and a few windows and some geraniums in pots
which couldn't even see the sun but still had huge heads.
Johnny helped me with a bag and we went under an arch
and along a stone passage to a door that was pinned back.
In spite of the ventilation the corridor beyond smelled of
garlic. A little table had a bell on it.

'There's no use ringing that thing,' Johnny said, then
bellowed. 'Mama!'

While we waited I had a look at the décor, which was
greenish. There were posters stuck on a board, some
illustrated, and all apparently advertisements for Macao's
cheaper entertainments.

'I can't talk to the old cow,' Johnny said. 'She has some
kind of English, but it's weird. Janey fixed things. *Mama!*'

The woman who came was not just fat, but distressingly
so, wearing a white apron marked with stains. She had
no chins, her face a continuation of solid neck. A moustache
matched thin black hair pulled back to a bun. I couldn't
guess at her blood strains or her age as she looked first
at me, then Johnny, then my suitcases. I tried Cantonese,
but nothing happened. Suddenly there was a rumble.

'What wanchee me side?'

It was pidgin, that old lingua franca of now almost
forgotten colonialism in China. In her youth, or some time,
the lady must have lived out of Macao, maybe Shanghai.
I've had no real training in this means of communication
but echoes of it reached me through Grandfather who was

an expert and always used it to his servants, even when he moved to Singapore.

'Me wanchee loom,' I said. 'Sleep, sleep.' I pointed to Johnny whom she seemed to have recognized. 'Flend.'

For half a minute the lady just continued staring, then her neck creased from a nod.

'Can do. Fixee topside.'

'Say, you made it,' Johnny said.

We bumped bags up a staircase to a landing where an open door advertised a bathroom which didn't appear to offer a coloured suite, and then up more stairs. The landlady used her fist to open the door of a room which seemed to be in an annex of its own, thumped into the apartment, then stood back to let us get a view of it.

On a sagging floor was a museum collection of simply tremendous bedroom furniture. I can't assign Portuguese periods but the stuff looked sixteenth or seventeenth century, four-poster bed with canopy, two enormous wardrobes, a chest at the foot of the bed, a couple of high-backed chairs with curved arms and on a table a ewer and washbasin set that looked like a majolica. The wood of the pieces was very dark from age and stain, and every square inch was carved.

I could imagine a grandee newly appointed as Governor sailing from Lisbon in his private three master, bringing with him all the domestic trimmings essential to maintain near viceregal pomp in the most remote of all Portugal's colonies after Timor. His second best bed made you very conscious of its probable history, some centuries of wild first nights, childbirth, marital boredom and formal death scenes with the family gathered around speculating, behind tears, as to who was to inherit what. It could easily have been the setting for a few murders. The proprietress turned down a cover that looked like quilted green moss, revealing white sheets and thumping feather pillows.

'Thisy good top top,' I said.

She came towards me holding out her hand palm uppermost in the international signal for payment in advance and I gave her two hundred escudos, at which she almost smiled.

'Is your room like this, too?' I asked Johnny.

He shook his head, a bit sour, as though he thought Janey and he should have been given the bridal suite.

'We've got to walk half a mile to that bathroom,' he said.

By the time I got to Macao's main post office business had started up again, the place full of people. Cantonese was all I needed to find my way about even though I couldn't read any of the notices, and at a desk I wrote out two signals. The one to Ranya read: 'REMOVED TO BOARDING HOUSE STOP NO TELEPHONE STOP ENJOYING SIMPLE TOURISM STOP DO NOT DISTURB LOVE PAUL.' The other was going to be much more expensive, to Ming Wa Chia, Business Consultants, who have the suitable cable address of 'alert'. 'INFORM SOONEST CABLE CARE CENTRAL POST OFFICE MACAO ALL AVAILABLE ON JOHN CASS ALLEGED EX US PEACE CORPS PHILIPPINES ALLEGED CURRENT REFUGEE WORKER KOWLOON STOP FOR INFORMATION SUGGEST CONTACT FATHER PELHAM KOWLOON STOP ALSO CHECK JANE DALY ALLEGED US BANK EMPLOYEE HONG KONG STOP DITTO AMELIA JACKSON ALLEGED US EXCHANGE TEACHER HONG KONG SIGNED PAUL HARRIS.'

I could have telephoned Ming Wa Chia Associates, but with no assurance that there wouldn't be a listening ear on the line, business consultants being particularly subject to this kind of interference. I have a theory, which has yet to let me down in practice, that the best defence against the proliferation of electronic interceptive devices is the old-fashioned uncoded telegram which these days no one ever imagines would be used for anything important.

There was a queue for my counter and I had to stand for twenty minutes, but when I reached the window I watched the clerk read my messages without interest, then count the words. I paid him and he gave me a box number for collecting the reply.

There were other queues. The longest, from the shabbiness of the people waiting in it, suggested some kind of social security benefit, if Macao has these. Three from the end was a man whose ears I would have recognized anywhere even though his head was turned away. It was Ho Tai.

CHAPTER VIII

In any jungle Teng's bodyguard could have followed me for as long as he liked, and within striking distance, without my being aware that he was there, but I didn't think he had much training in city work. I went out of the post office, hired a taxi, saw Ho Tai getting into another, tipped my driver for an emergency stop in traffic, left the car to run up a lane and then down another which brought me back into the shopping street, crossing this to a men's clothing store. I took my time over a choice of three handkerchiefs after which I pretended an interest in a rack of ties designed for the older man who still feels a boy at heart, which I don't. The display windows gave me a good view but there was no sign of my tail. Later, out in sunshine again, I checked all shadow for a loitering figure, not seeing one, which didn't mean that Ho Tai wasn't in the area. I went to a café which had tables in shade under a series of stone arches, choosing a chair back against a wall. I could see well up and down the street. A waiter brought me beer.

The tables and chairs took up all the pavement in the café's section of this semi arcade, forcing strollers to detour it via the road and, when there were cars passing out there, practically pushing them into the gutter. I saw Amelia Jackson when she was still quite some distance away and watched a slow approach in which her attention was divided between shop windows and life. She was carrying a fairly big and awkwardly shaped parcel suggesting a visit to one of the many little antique shops doing a good line in pretending that they hadn't heard tourism has come to Macao, offering pieces of what just might be dusty Ming but are actually in mass production from a Canton factory. She was wearing the seersucker in which I had first seen her and an expression that seemed just slightly tinged with sadness. A car forced her into the gutter within feet of my table.

'Hallo.'

She jumped, then turned her head. I must have been mistaken about the sadness, she was now looking like an active member of the Boonville Methodist Ladies' Guild.

'Won't you join me for a cool drink?'

'No, thank you, Mr Harris.'

That was crisp.

'I'd like a talk.'

'I can't think why.'

'Sit down!'

'What?'

I was on my feet, pulling out a chair. I didn't actually push her into it, but I helped.

'Really, I don't think . . .'

'What can I order?'

'I don't want anything. Well . . . do you suppose they have any English tea?'

'I doubt it. Coca-Cola?'

'All right.'

I shouted the order. Miss Jackson's parcel was on the

table. She added her handbag, pulled off a glove, then appeared surprised to find she had done this.

'I have something to explain,' I said.

'There's no need to explain anything, Mr Harris.'

'You had a talk with da Silva?'

'Yes, I did.'

'Quite a lurid story.'

'You might call it that.'

She was looking down the street. The Coca-Cola arrived, and I paid for it.

'You also heard that I had been chucked out of the hotel?'

'Yes.'

She went on looking down the street. Then she sucked in a long breath.

'You probably think I'm a bigoted old woman, Mr Harris. Well, I don't believe I am. If you want to know what I really thought . . . well . . . it was the kind of girl you chose.'

'She *was* a bit grubby,' I said.

I expected that would make her turn her head and it did.

'I met that girl out on the Praya. She had been thrown out of a car, apparently by clients. I gave her a few escudos but it wasn't a down payment on anything. When she realized this there was a bit of a fracas, during which she stole my wallet. I haven't seen her since. I don't know how she got into my bedroom.'

Amelia was staring at me like a schoolteacher trained in the art of getting the truth out of a pupil, even when this doesn't come easily.

'If she stole your wallet why didn't you go to the police?'

'The girl returned it to the hotel. Pretending I had left it when I was with her. Didn't da Silva tell you that?'

'No, he didn't. And I just don't understand.'

'Neither do I, yet.'

She didn't believe my story and I didn't really feel that she wanted to. It could be that for the first time in her life she had been able to identify, in spite of the façade of near gentility he wore in public, a totally sex-obsessed male. As such I had been classified, a travel experience. Never again would she accept a reasonably pleasant manner at its face value. If her defensive reaction to sitting at a table with me was an act it was a good one. I had the feeling that if I touched her arm she would scream.

'I'm just a shade suspicious of you, too,' I said.

Her eyes widened.

'And just what could you mean by that?'

'I get a bit jumpy when anyone moves in close to me suddenly. And you picked me up on that ferry.'

'I *what*?'

'It seemed that way to me. And the CIA could be using exchange schoolteachers these days. After all it's beautiful cover.'

'I don't know what you're talking about? The CIA?'

'US Central Intelligence Agency.'

She picked up the Coca-Cola and had not just one sip but three. Then she put the glass down again.

'This is just crazy!'

'A lot crazier things are happening all around us. The Far East is melodrama. It has been ever since World War Two.'

'But *me*!'

'You're intelligent, you're observant, and you make contact with people easily. Further, you might have taken on the job just for the hell of it.'

'The . . . *hell* of it?'

'Why not?'

Her flush then couldn't have been an act. People can't flush to order. Amelia Jackson was flattered. She opened her handbag, took out a handkerchief, blew her nose

briskly, then put the handkerchief back. A catch snapped.
She said :

'I shall certainly remember Macao.' I got a long look.
'Why would the CIA be interested in you?'

'They have a complex about it.'

'With reason?'

'Well, maybe once or twice they've had a reason.'

'Who *are* you?'

'Just what I said. A business man. Every now and then
I'm forced to be a little unconventional. Due to the area
in which I operate.'

'Little things like disappearing for two days?'

'It makes people curious.'

'I'm not surprised. Unconventional couldn't mean criminal?'

'That's harsh, Amelia. Do I look like a crook?'

'In the books I read they never do.'

'In real life most villains look like villains. Ask any
policeman.'

'You don't want to tell me what you're doing?'

'I might risk it even though I haven't read your
dossier yet.'

'My *what*?'

'I've just sent away to Hong Kong for it.'

'I don't believe that.'

But she wanted to.

'I'll let you see what my inquiry service says about
you when I get their report.'

'Paul Harris, you're fooling me, and don't think I don't
know it. Where did you go when you walked out of the
hotel that night? Somewhere in this town?'

'No. I was escorted to a yacht.'

'That's not a very probable story.'

'One reason I didn't use it on da Silva. I didn't think
he was the right audience.'

'But I am?'

'Yes.'

'Why?'

'I think you'll give me the benefit of the doubt.'

She picked up the Coca-Cola again.

'If you're mocking me . . .'

'I'm not. Let's go and have a look at Camoens's cave.'

'Now?'

'There's a couple of hours of daylight still. You didn't think of going on your own?'

'No.'

In gathering up her possessions she dropped a glove. I picked it up.

'I don't know why I wear these in a hot climate,' she said.

'So you won't leave fingerprints, of course.'

Amelia looked at me for all of half a minute before she began to laugh. In the taxi I found that she had been reading up about Camoens.

'He really had a terrible time, Paul. All kinds of things. Just awful. He was shipwrecked and then put in jail, but he just went on writing whatever happened. He seems to have been a real genius. I ought to have read him but I've never even seen any of his books. I guess they must be translated. I'll look into this when I get back to the States. Have you read him?'

'No.'

'Like so many writers he wasn't properly appreciated until he was dead.'

'That happens to a lot of us who aren't writers.'

The botanic gardens were really very beautiful, lush, almost tropical, but with more foliage than colour. It looked to me a great place for snakes but I didn't see any. We seemed to be the only customers, though there was no difficulty in finding our way to the cave; dead writers get signposted.

I got hot and took off my jacket, shoving my wallet with passport inside it into the hip pocket of my trousers. The cave wasn't really very impressive, on the shallow side, and though I had half expected to find it furnished with Portuguese antiques, it wasn't, not even an upended orange box for a table. We had to guess where Camoens had sat waiting for his muse to fly in, like Elijah waiting for the ravens. There was a smell of damp.

'Amelia, it's time you let me carry that parcel.'

'No, I'm fine the way I am, thank you.'

She hadn't told me what was in it, perhaps now a little uneasy about her impulse buying. She stood clutching brown paper looking around at what the world does to its great artists.

'It's sort of sad, isn't it, Paul? I don't suppose there is anything as hard as leading the creative life.'

I could have suggested that business executives have it harder and die younger, but I kept quiet. After homage we went back amongst the boulders, reaching an area of tree ferns where the path narrowed and I let her go on ahead.

There wasn't a sound from behind before a strike at the base of my skull. The abattoir blow put me on my knees, with vision out of focus. I shoved out arms to keep from going down flat and for seconds stayed humped over like a dazed quadruped. Amelia let out a weird thin noise and there was a shout that wasn't from her. I lifted my head and could make out white trousers running away from us. Amelia was standing with a piece of limp paper held in both hands. On the path was her handbag, its contents scattered and about her feet were fragments of something I couldn't identify.

'Paul! Are you hurt? Oh . . .!'

It wasn't easy to stand, but I made it.

'You . . .?'

'He never touched me. He was trying to get away when I hit him.'

'You *what*?'

'With my vase.'

The star of this action certainly wasn't me. Amelia's straw hat was slightly askew but otherwise she looked ready for round two. It was my hope there wouldn't be one because I wasn't. I knew myself for a fool on two counts, first to think I had shaken off Ho Tai, second bringing her to the one place in Macao which could give him full scope for his specialist talents.

'Did that man hit you on the head, Paul?'

'Neck. It'll be sore for a couple of days, that's all.'

The karate chop had been nicely measured to stun.

'Your knees! There's blood coming through the cloth.'

'Just grazing.'

'It looks worse than that. But he didn't get your wallet. He dropped it.'

'Was that after you hit him?'

'I suppose so. I'm not very sure. You haven't lost anything out of it?'

I had lost my passport. It seemed best not to tell her. I helped her shove things into the handbag, though bending made me dizzy.

'Sorry about your vase.'

'It wasn't any good. I knew that right after I bought it. Paul, are you really all right?'

'Of course.'

Walking was a bit painful, but I managed not to hobble. When the gates and our waiting taxi were in sight I said:

'Give you a stout stick and you'd get through Central Park alone at night.'

Suddenly her colour wasn't good. There was a bench and she sat on it.

'Oh, my,' she said, in a small voice.

I grabbed her bag and pushed her head well down. It was

all of a minute before she straightened.

'That was silly.'

'Perfectly natural.'

She tried to smile.

'I'm sure CIA women don't go faint.'

We found our driver asleep along the front seat so there was no point in asking him if he had seen a running man. Amelia sat in the car with her eyes shut.

'We'd better go straight to the police,' she said, without opening them.

'I'll deal with that side. I'm taking you to the hotel.'

She didn't speak again until we had drawn up in front of the Algarve.

'You're coming in to let me fix up those knees.'

'The management wouldn't allow you to take me through the lobby.'

'I'd like to see them try to stop me.'

'Elastoplast is all I need.'

I helped her out. She seemed fine again.

'Amelia, will you do something for me? I've sent my co-director in Singapore a cable, but she may still ring this hotel to find out why I've left it. I'd hate her to hear da Silva's story.'

'She might believe it?'

'More than likely. Tell the desk that all calls for me are to be switched to your room.'

'Isn't your co-director going to think that strange?'

'You're my temporary secretary.'

'I see. What's her name?'

'Mrs Nivalahannanda. I'm out if she calls but you're taking all messages.'

'How do I deliver them?'

'We're lunching together tomorrow. The Solmar restaurant. Quarter to one.'

'I'll look forward to that. Will you have my dossier from Hong Kong by then?'

'I might. Try not to think about what happened.'

'I'm not going to think about it.'

'Good. Why not take that prescription you issued to me, an early night?'

She shook her head.

'No. After dinner I'm going down to the casino. To gamble. Ten dollars' worth.'

She started up the steps, then turned.

'I know you're not going to the police, Paul. You recognized that man, didn't you?'

I watched her to the hotel entrance, then got back in the taxi.

A chemist supplied the Elastoplast and also stuck it on my knees, making half English noises as he did this about the state of Macao's roads, how they ought to have all those cobbles up and asphalt laid. Dark had dropped on the city when I came out into the streets again. I heard what I took for a motor-cycle without a silencer, then recognized rotors clattering in a take-off. K. K. Long was leaving, probably with my passport in his pocket. Getting hold of a replacement was going to be a matter of days at least and until I had that document I was stuck in a Portuguese colony, under detention in an area of six square miles.

I rang Teng's fortress where a woman answered in vague and distant sounding Cantonese, informing me that her master was in bed with a high temperature and couldn't be disturbed on any account, a clear case of diplomatic illness. Since there was no chance at all I'd be allowed through the gate of the villa, and a hacksaw on it might get me electrocuted, I made another call, this time to Ramundo P. Alvares. He wasn't in his offices, but I left a message suggesting that if he was free to dine with me this evening I would be delighted to meet him at the Solmar restaurant at eight p.m. Then I went walking, to ease a stiffness in my neck and work off a soreness in my knees, doing routine practice checks along the way to see if I was tailed. It was obvious that I had allowed old skills at evading pursuit to rust and an hour or two in Macao's old quarter left me with a deep respect for the cover it offered, even the main streets having nearly complete paths of shadow and with plenty of dark lanes available for use as observation posts.

Mr Alvares was not waiting for me in the restaurant and at twenty past eight I decided he had preferred a girl-friend, letting the head waiter lead me to one of those tables reserved for the customer who doesn't matter, in an almost dark corner just beyond the door to the kitchen. This kept swinging back and forth to let me hear the cries of chefs under stress. The waiter looking after my district was an old man who wanted to retire but couldn't afford the luxury, sad and slow, an exile from the big tipping. He warmed to me somewhat when I said I knew nothing about Portuguese cooking and put myself in his hands. My first course was a fish I couldn't begin to identify, probably old carp, but in a delicious sauce.

A commotion made me look up. My guest had arrived, located me, and was outraged at the indignity of a table in outer darkness. The head waiter looked in shock, Alvares was big here. Both advanced with arms waving.

'My dear Mr Harris, I am so sorry I am late. Please forgive. The delay was unavoidable. And I have been complaining about this table. You should never have been placed here. If only you had mentioned my name. But another will be made ready for us.'

He pointed out towards the people who ran the colony, quite a few of them smoking cheroots with their soup courses.

'I like this waiter,' I said.

There is nothing like kitchen noise for security cover and as host I had the last word. Eventually my guest sat down, bitter about this banishment from the prestige zone,

the heat from his resentment sending over waves of scent
only recently sprayed on. An apéritif calmed him but I got
a bit bored during his performance with the menu card,
real gourmet stuff, every item discussed volubly in a mix of
Portuguese and Chinese, many suggested dishes loudly rejected, presumably because they were too cheap.

'Have you ordered your next course, Mr Harris?'

'I'm leaving everything to the waiter.'

He was shocked.

'Oh, no, no, you mustn't do that! Let me suggest the
veal? I've decided on it myself. It comes from China and
is usually excellent.'

The price of that meat covered a heavy surcharge as the
result of all the risks it ran getting over from Red territory,
the night's top feature for fat wallets.

'Veal it is,' I said, with dogged amiability.

The wine list got ten minutes to itself. He looked at me
over it.

'What's that you're drinking?'

'The rosé of the house.'

He shrugged, then turned up the palms of his hands.

'Perhaps I will have a bottle of Chambertin?'

'By all means.'

With the vital decisions about what was to go into his
stomach made he was able to sit back, sipping sherry,
and directed towards me a very generous ration of charm.
He was a talented conversationalist, that great art of being
able to fill a vacuum with words, and he appeared to have
forgotten the slightly strained note on which our previous
contact had ended. Yesterdays were nothing to him, he
came to each new day with a slate wiped clean of old dis-
tresses, and the ability to do this, especially if you're a
lawyer, is yet another great gift. He was probably invincibly attractive to many women from sexual emanations put
out, like the musk he also used, but this didn't sell him to
me. Even in a poor light I could see that he hadn't shaved

after office hours, which probably meant that a rushed
visit to one of his girl-friends had already been part of his
evening. He was certainly hungry now, and when the hors-
d'oeuvres came he put an immense amount on his plate.

Alvares probed around my recent absence from Macao
which I admitted without going into any details. There
was no need for explanations, I was certain he knew not
only where I had been, but how I had travelled, out via
a Colt in the spine, back via helicopter.

'Mr Harris, that matter you raised with me . . . are you
proceeding with it?'

'No.'

One might have expected the cancellation of that huge
fee to have troubled him more than it appeared to; he
seemed positively relieved.

'You have reconsidered?'

'Yes. Changes in my affairs have altered the situation.'

'Ah!'

He looked wise, then sent me a smile which twinkled. I
think he considered offering congratulations on my decision to become one of the boys but decided to wait
until the common ground between us had been more fully
explored. He lifted a fork loaded with three sardines
and a considerable portion of potato salad with garlic and
chewed, looking at me as though I had suddenly become
someone for whom he would now feel considerable affec-
tion.

I didn't think the news that I was joining the team, relayed first to Teng Ching Wok and then radioed to Long
on the *Hui Yang*, was going to get me my passport back
in the morning, but it would probably mean that intense
surveillance of my activities would be called off. I wanted
that. Hauntings by Ho Tai had become oppressive and I
knew that in Alvares I could be certain of a reliable message
boy.

'In the new situation which has developed, Mr Harris, there is perhaps some way I can assist you?'

He couldn't wait for it, he had to know.

'There may be.'

'In that case I am available for consultation whenever you wish.'

It was time to fly my kite.

'The registration of the OSL ships here in Macao interests me,' I said. 'In view of the fact that this isn't a deep water port.'

His face showed nothing.

'You see, Mr Alvares, I am faced with increasing problems with my Hok Lin ships registered in Singapore. Costs are spiralling. Profit margins are threatened. I'm being forced to consider the idea of using a convenience port, just as Mr Long does with his main fleet.'

Alvares remained perfectly serene at this first use between us of the sacred name.

'Panama or Liberia are fine for someone who works his ships around the world, but my operations so far are limited to the Far East. It might be against my other interests in Singapore to have my registration so far afield. You get my point?'

'But of course.'

'Then you'll understand why I'm more than a little curious about Mr Long's reasons for registering his proxy line here. Why not Panama for OSL, too?'

'You didn't discuss this with him?'

We were really coming out into the open.

'No. I thought you were the right man to give me a lead here.'

Flattery gets you a long way. Alvares leaned forward 'Just what do you want to know, Mr Harris?'

I inserted a timed pause, then hissed across the table:

'Is Macao now in the process of becoming a rival convenience port to Panama and Liberia?'

His reaction was a sad disappointment. He stared at me, unable to conceal startled surprise. As a man with a finger on the pulse of this colony he wasn't going to admit that he knew nothing, but this was clearly written on his face. My kite flying had been a flop. He rallied a bit with a poor bid to look mysterious, but all he managed to say was:

'It is a possibility.'

I sat back in my chair. What I had suggested seemed much more than just a possibility to me. The Orient, with its new crop of shipping tycoons, is rapidly becoming the world centre for marine haulage and it seems only a matter of time until we have our own convenience port. Why should Chinese shipowners have to register in the Western Hemisphere in order to keep down running costs? A kind of new area patriotism comes into this, too, the Far East for Far Easterners in all things.

Hong Kong might seem the logical port for conversion to this use, but any bid to do that would result in howls of world protest, the place already celebrated for an economic survival based on low costs from sweated labour. No British government could ever contemplate that particular expansion of the colony's commercial interests no matter how lucrative it might prove. The Portuguese, however, have never paid the slightest attention to what the world thinks of them and in this role Macao would become a big revenue earner for their empire that has so miraculously survived against great odds even though pieces of it have been nicked off here and there. The fact that none of the vessels registered in Macao could ever enter their official home port wouldn't matter in the least, not one in a hundred of the ships registered in Liberia have even been near Monrovia.

Alvares had staged a comeback from near shock.

'You heard talk of this in Singapore, perhaps?'

'No,' I said, almost surly.

'A hint from Mr Long?'

'Nothing remotely like that.'

He didn't believe me. I had started a rumour that was going to snowball. It would be all around this city by morning and the day after the economic seismographs of the many Hong Kong stock exchanges would be vibrating. The outlook for Oriental shipping companies which had issued stock would suddenly seem even brighter than it was, their shares leaping up by a dollar. Next week they would fall again by a dollar and a half. This didn't disturb me at all. I was troubled only by no confirmation of my suspicions. If Long was playing this card he had, as usual, held his hand close in to his chest.

Alvares was now having great difficulty in controlling excitement. If he had been planning to go on from dinner with me to another of his girl-friends he was now cancelling this in favour of using the telephone in his role as the local in-man. The ultimate result of his activity could be Long sacking another minor stooge which would see me doing a useful piece of work, but not one that in any way advantaged my interests.

We parted outside the restaurant with a handshake and I went to see an Italian film. The theatre was three quarters empty and the picture so sensitive to a setting utterly remote from this one that half-way through it I fell asleep, woken only by the national anthem, a custom still clung to in the last colonies.

When I got back to the Castello Bianco the silence inside the boarding house was like wool padding. I listened for a while on the landing, a dead quiet hard to accept in this crowded part of the city. Beyond a stone arched passage leading to a front door the pavements were crowded with strollers and yet this place was as much an oasis of preserved silence as one of those mini estates up on the hills.

I went up the last short flight to my room, groped for a handle, opened the door, fumbled again for a bulbous

light switch and clicked down the protruding lever crown-
ing it. A single, unshaded forty-candle power bulb put no
great strain on the Macao electricity supply, leaving many
shadows, but almost at once I saw that the sampan girl
had decided it was time I stopped sleeping alone.

CHAPTER IX

The girl had been smoking, there was a strong smell of
acrid Chinese tobacco, but was now lying on the huge
bed with her arms thrown back over her head. She was
still wearing blue denim, trousers and top, and her make-
up was still garish. Sleep hadn't returned her to innocence.

I put my jacket over the arm of a chair, then went to
the window, a decaying wooden casement which protested
against being opened. I turned to find my visitor sliding
off the bed, wary as a stray cat. I remembered those claws
as she edged along the mattress to one of the bottom posts
holding up the canopy. She slid her hand around this and
watched me. Someone had to say something.

'Come for your reward?'

She shook her head. Any prettiness she had was painted
on to a broad face with flattened features, her mouth
coloured to a fullness it didn't have. She was short even
with platform-soled shoes strapped to ankles under the
trousers and, though slim, gave no suggestion of frailty. In
bare feet she would stay anchored to a bouncing deck by
muscled calves and strong thighs.

'What's your name?'

'Wei Linfen.'

'Are you a refugee?'

She nodded.

'If you're not after money what do you want?'

She didn't answer.

'You'd better sit down.'

She let go of the post to perch on the carved chest, straight-backed and directly under the light. Except for plastered make-up the girl was clean tonight, clean hands, clean denims, and no hint of cheap perfume. She wore no jewellery, black hair straight back to the traditional bun. But for that painted face she could have been a harbour coolie's hard-working wife.

'You've got a cigarette?' she asked. 'I've smoked mine.'

'Only a cigar.'

'That'll do.'

She lit it herself, matches from a tunic pocket, careful to get the tip glowing, inhaling at once. I sat down in one of the viceregal chairs, conscious of its high back rising behind me like a judge's throne, and conscious, too, of my questions as authoritarian, these a despatch from the invincibly secure towards the inevitably underprivileged.

'When did you come from China?'

'Nearly two years ago.'

'You had to go on the streets?'

'I could have worked in a factory.'

'Then why not?'

'There's more money in this.'

'Even for a boat girl?'

'I don't live on a boat any more. I've a room.'

She was going up in the world.

Her story came easily enough, but it wasn't quite what I was expecting, no bid for sympathy via a mother, father and six brothers all left in Canton and all dependent on what she sent them to eke out a miserable existence since her father had lost his job as a high school teacher during the cultural revolution. It was interesting that she wasn't out to break my heart, apparently having left China because it bored her, about the best reason for leaving any place. Echoes from the world beyond the puritan socialism had reached that Canton men's underwear factory and she had wanted to have a look at the total decadence the propaganda medias kept urging her to scorn. I didn't get the feeling that Macao had disillusioned her at all, she took pride in her work and to get from a sampan to a room with her looks meant that she must be technically highly skilled.

'Was that your pimp who pushed you out of the car?'

Her small eyes widened.

'I don't have a pimp! I don't need one.'

'Who then?'

'I told you! They didn't pay me.'

'Nonsense! The whole thing was staged. The man you were with didn't want my money, just a look at what was in my wallet. Your cut was the money.'

'I don't know about that.'

'You mean you hadn't seen him before that night?'

She shrugged and looked at the floor. She wasn't going to identify anyone, even for a price, the risk factor to her too great. Macao has that handy current to keep murder statistics low because no bodies are found.

'You haven't told me why you're here?'

She smiled at a silly question. She had the good teeth which come from a diet low in meat protein, though these were a bit on the sharp side, more than her incisors pointed.

'To give you pleasure,' she said.

'And after we've had our pleasure?'

'You'll help me.'

'To do what?'

'Go to Singapore.'

'Why should I?'

'When you've had me you'll want me often.'

'Badly enough to pay for your ticket south?'

She nodded. There is nothing like having complete professional confidence.

'Why do you want to go to Singapore?'

I was half expecting to be told that the hourly rates were much better down where I live, but it wasn't that, apparently even a girl as busy as she was takes time off to have a dream. She might have been a resident in the Bronx longing for Florida. I raised a few snags, including our immigration laws which have no loopholes for refugees without influence, but it turned out that I was to be that influence, a man really fulfilled for the first time under her ministrations who would take to her like an addiction. And I was rich, she knew that from the credit cards in my wallet. It is astonishing how the credit card has caught on all over the world, already you can use them in the better houses in Bangkok, debited next month for this month's joy. My authority is Ranya.

In her way the girl was quite appealing, no nonsense about how she meant to turn over a new leaf down south via learning shorthand and typing. When you've acquired a real skill in this life you stick to it. It was just a new scene she wanted.

'If I'd been a man,' she said, 'I'd have been out of here long ago.'

'You mean to Hong Kong?'

'No.'

'Without a passport how do you get beyond Hong Kong?'

'You go to the ships.'

'A job on a junk?'

'No, the big ships.'

There was a ticking in my brain like the sound of a kitchen alarm clock. I got up, found a flask in a suitcase, and filled the cap cup.

'This is whisky. Would you like some?'

She nodded, reaching out with both hands, fingernails tonight unpainted. I drank from the flask, saying half over a shoulder:

'Where are these ships?'

'Taiwan.'

It was what I expected to hear. I turned.

'Your refugee men go to them from here?'

K

'Yes.'

'Many?'

She nodded.

'How do you know about this?'

'All the sampan people know about it.'

'It sounds easy. Is it?'

'If you're a man and the right age. And especially if you were a fisherman in China. They want men who are used to the sea.'

'How are these men recruited?'

'Every now and then someone comes here to tell them about life on the big ships.'

'You mean the recruiting is done openly?'

'It's done amongst the refugees and boat people, if that's what you mean.'

'With police knowledge?'

'The police don't bother with the water people more than they have to. They leave them alone unless there's real trouble. A hundred refugees could leave Macao in a night and the police wouldn't know or care. There are always new people coming in.'

'Not nearly so many as there used to be, I'm told.'

'That's what you're told. They're still coming. The camps are still full. So are those shanty villages. The police don't go near them after dark.'

'But the agents from Taiwan do? Have you heard one of them talking?'

'They don't talk to women.'

Wei Linfen had managed to skip both the refugee camps and the shanty villages on her arrival from China, this by the simple expedient of giving pleasure to two brothers amongst the boat people. They made room for her on their sampan even though they had their old mother on board to do the cooking. This domesticity had lasted for six months until one of the brothers had gone to the ships and the other had got the idea of exploiting Miss Wei's one talent commercially. She didn't see why her lover should get the profits from this, so left him, renting space on another sampan. Real success had earned her a room in town and from then she had never looked back. I suspected that the blue denims tonight were for my benefit, her usual working uniform these days more likely to be a split-to-the-hip cheongsam.

I gave her another whisky and then pumped in the questions. She seemed quite willing to answer them though her replies were short, sometimes monosyllabic; but a picture built up. It was rumoured that the recruits for the Taiwan ships were taken first to a training vessel, a sort of floating technical college, though no one really knew, for the men who had gone didn't seem to write home. Nor did they come back to Macao to visit relations. Money sometimes reached the relatives who had been left behind but apparently no coloured postcards from exotic foreign parts, as though part of those contracts signed was a clause insisting that they slice away their old lives completely. In terms of Macao they had just disappeared, almost as if their bodies had been thrown into that current which swept past beyond the anchorage.

I didn't ask Wei Linfen whether she knew the name of the Taiwan company which was doing such fine undercover in relieving the refugee pressure on this city. I refilled her cup, then sat down to think about K. K. Long's phenomenal rise since his purchase of that first aged ship. He had hit on a contemporary equivalent of the press gang, an unlimited supply of men coming from China without passports or papers, not even having identities which could be formally established. All they had brought with them was hope and this wore thin fast, making them highly receptive to that Taiwan sales pitch. Signing on did nothing to give them any basic human rights under any country's laws, just confirmed their permanent statelessness, which meant that later they couldn't hope to escape in one of the ports their KKL ship visited. Long Kin could pay them what he liked and treat them as he liked, without having any worries about the threat of labour troubles. No wonder he had massive plans for expansion and could face prolonged price wars with such equanimity, no problem about crewing for the new ships, he just signed on more refugees and intensified training schedules on his floating polytechnic.

Miss Wei had been remarkably patient, as though quite used to irrelevancies of this kind before she was able to demonstrate her skills. Also, my whisky had mellowed her, it was quite clear she liked it. It was a good malt but it hadn't mellowed me. I remembered the cabin of that cruiser with its permanent reek from a traffic in human flesh.

Suddenly I was offered a total surprise. The girl had put down her cup and with the agility of a trained gymnast, if not actually a contortionist, she shoved her legs straight out in front of her, heels three feet off the floor. She stayed that way, too, for quite some time, balanced on her bottom which the carving on the chest must have made painful, her hands palm together under her chin as though for the Indian greeting. Then very slowly, her knees came up, a splendidly synchronized display of muscular co-ordination until she was looking at me between them. I got her little fox smile. On a perfectly even breath she said :
'We make sex now?'

In spite of this remarkable piece of advertising I felt it wisest to refuse, having learned at Grandfather's knee that you pay for a whore twice, once at the time and then again later to your doctor. I offered fifty escudos' solace money and she was amiable enough, not pressing on to defeat my shyness, as though experience had taught her all about male rhythms in these matters. Further, I held out the prospect of future contact by asking for her address. She wrote this down on a piece of paper I provided, saying that all I had to do was hand it to any taxi-driver. It seemed to me that she had a very practised hand with the character squiggles for an ex-Canton factory girl, but China is now totally literate, or almost. From the door I was sent that smile again. She was very quiet on creaking stairs.

In that canopied bed I couldn't switch off my brain for sleep. I read recently about a well-known dictator admitted to hospital suffering from hypermania. That sounds like a mental condition likely to put a man permanently out of politics but apparently it isn't anything nearly so serious, just a mind running away on wild revs its owner can't reduce because the throttle mechanism has jammed wide open. The cure is prolonged sedation. I had none available and when I did get drowsy a stab of pain from my neck had me wide awake again.

There was no dawn chorus of birds, just a domestic row from a room across the courtyard, this coming from a couple who seemed to be reviewing their relationship in some detail, both bitter. I was backing the girl to win, her lamentations had reached quite a screech, when there was a crash of crockery. Silence after that was unnerving, and it could be that the police would soon be investigating one of Macao's rare official murders. All of twenty minutes later, and from the same source, there was laughter, male and female, a little duet of it like something out of a Mozart opera, a sudden, sprightly expression of deep joy. I lay alone, a man deprived of these little spaces of domestic bliss which make the rest endurable, trying to imagine Ranya laughing like that, but just not able to hear her doing it.

At seven-thirty I got up, wanting a hot bath. I put on a robe and went down the flight to the landing. Just as I reached it a door opened and out came Miss Jane Daly wearing a kimono covered in brightly coloured morning glories. She looked at me for seconds, as though groping for the right thing to say to a crypto-fascist in the early morning outside a bathroom, then hit on it exactly.

'The heater thing isn't working. There's no hot water.'

She went down a passage walking like a girl who has recently spent a morbid couple of days at a Marilyn Monroe festival of remembrance. I went in and filled a stained tub with cold water and sat in it, never actually lying back, just splashing the rest of me. The soap I had brought from Singapore wouldn't lather properly.

Breakfast was three cups of coffee and a couple of Portuguese imitation croissants in a café that was ten degrees chillier than the pavement outside. To get circulation going again I walked fast to the central post office, produced my box number and was handed a signal.

'JOHN CASS NO CONNECTION KOWLOON REFUGEES STOP UNKNOWN TO FATHER PELHAM STOP UNKNOWN MANILA STOP TWO WEEKS HONG KONG BOARDING HOUSE APPARENTLY TOURISM STOP DALY SACKED US BANK LOCAL OFFICE FOR MARXIST PROPAGANDA STAFF STOP REGARDED UNDESIRABLE ALIEN DEPORTATION IMMINENT ON RETURN HONG KONG STOP JACKSON OKAY US EXCHANGE TEACHER ON AVAILABLE EVIDENCE SIGNED MING.'

I tore the cable into small pieces, put it in a waste bin, then had a careful look around for Ho Tai who didn't seem to be on my tail so early, but I checked this during my climb up a hill to see the carvings done by Japanese on a ruined church. I wasn't followed.

The saints on that façade all looked like Orientals, which was reasonable enough considering the number of Japanese Christian martyrs there had been under Iyeyasu and his son in the seventeenth century. There was something sad about those lasting memorials to a little group of displaced persons who have left no other trace on history, and I walked down into the town again thinking about the astonishing stubbornness of the Nipponese once they have committed themselves to any course, be this practical or emotional. Thirty thousand of them died because they refused to spit on the symbol of the Cross, and but for a couple of dictators Japan might today have been nominally a Christian country, as is the Philippines.

At the Solmar I was this time given a table well clear of the tourist reservation and with a good view of the entrance. Amelia Jackson was fifteen minutes late and arrived looking worried, taking a moment or two to spot me and work her way over. She sat down without in the least suggesting someone about to add another travel experience to her bulging store of these. Then she remembered duty as a guest to say in a preoccupied way :

'This is a cute place.' She opened her bag. 'I have a message from your lady in Singapore. I wrote down what she told me to.'

'What time did she call?'

'About ten. I guess she *was* ringing to find out why you had moved. She certainly seemed concerned about that.'

The note contained undertones of something stronger than concern for my well-being.

Even if you have no phone you can call me. Do that tomorrow. *Most* important. Ralph P. Brinkhausen called again from Texas. *Must* have instructions.

I put the slip in my pocket.

'How did she react to my having a new secretary?'

Amelia continued to look serious.

'Not well. She asked a lot of questions. Terribly curious about who I was. I said I was going around the world taking odd jobs.'

'Near enough the truth.'

'Not near enough for me, Paul.' Her voice was sharp. 'I'm not good at deceiving people. In the end I had to tell her how old I am.'

'You think she believed you?'

'No. She said I didn't sound that old. She's quite a fierce woman.'

'She has a good opinion of herself.'

'Possessive of you, I'd say. Has she ideas?'

'Yes.'

'And how do you react to them?'

'Mostly no. Except in my weak moments.'

Amelia didn't smile.

'I see. Don't you ever think of settling?'

'Not often.'

She still wore her solemn expression.

'Maybe I can understand that. I've never been a good sharer, either. I had an apartment once with another teacher. She was very nice, but I just can't get along with other people's habits. So I'm an old maid.'

'Bachelor girl.'

'Not at my time of life.'

The waiter came. I suggested a sherry but Amelia frowned that away. We ordered soup, something that sounded as though it was a chowder. Amelia put some butter on a bread stick and munched this.

'How did the gambling go?' I asked.

She swallowed.

'I don't think I want to talk about it.'

'Why not?'

'It's just something I don't want to remember, that's all.'

Service was good, the waiter arrived with our soup. Amelia asked for a glass of ice water, then looked straight at me.

'I lost one hundred and forty-seven dollars.'

'What?'

'No fool like an old fool.'

'But what happened?'

'What do you think happened? I just went mad, that's all.'

'Amelia . . .?'

'I know what you're going to say. I'll say it for myself. I went down with ten dollars out of my purse. Actually, I had it in my hand. That was all I was going to use. For an experience.'

I waited.

'I won thirty dollars in the first half-hour.'

'Roulette?'

'I guess so. It had a wheel. And a ball. I began to see numbers in my mind. Paul, it was quite awful. As if I believed in those numbers! So I backed them. I mean, I went on doing it. Even when I was losing. Nothing like this has ever happened to me; I've never even had shares on the market, I just use the savings account. I feel as if I had lost all moral sense.'

'That's ridiculous.'

'No, it's not. At my table there was an old Chinese woman. Her clothes weren't even clean, she was that poor. I think we saw her before. She had no money to speak of, and never has had, but she was gambling what she had got hold of somewhere that day. And I stood near her and went on doing it, too. It was like a . . . a mania. The awful thing is that I could go down again and do it tonight. Part of me wants to. Paul, it's a vice, just like drugs. And I could be swept off like that, in just one little experiment.'

I had a spoonful of soup.

'I didn't sleep at all,' Amelia said. 'I kept seeing that old woman. And then seeing myself. I was another person down there, a person I hadn't met before. It frightened me to think of it. I know you probably want to laugh, but no part of me does.'

The waiter came back to ask if we liked our soup. Amelia tested hers and said it was lovely. When the man had gone she said :

'I could stay and face this out, but I'm not going to.'

'What do you mean?'

'I'm getting on tonight's boat back to Hong Kong. And what that means is that I haven't the moral stamina to stay on in a hotel with a casino down on the ground floor. I'm a coward, too.'

'You're not.'

'Yes, I am. And if you're going to say that because I hit that man with my vase I have courage, that's just nonsense. It was a reflex action, that's all, nothing I had to think about. And I went weak after it.'

'Everyone gets a shock reaction to violence.'

'You're trying to be kind to me, Paul. I can't be kind to myself. I don't need kindness. It was the Apostle with your name who told us about keeping the beast in us under control.'

'You haven't got a beast in you, Amelia.'

'Yes, I have too. I found that out last night. Maybe this will be good for me. I thought I had myself all defined and everything. Well, I was wrong. I'm just as susceptible to temptation as anyone else. And I'm catching that boat.'

She opened her handbag, blew her nose briskly, put the handkerchief back and snapped the catch. Then she finished her soup. Both the waiter and I tried to interest her in the last course, but food was just food, something you needed to keep going but couldn't allow to become an end in itself. She decided on fish. In a bid to brighten things up I said :

'I've had that signal on you.'

'What?'

'Your dossier.'

'Oh, Paul, you know I don't believe in that.'

'It said : "Jackson okay US Exchange teacher on avail-

able evidence". That last phrase seems significant to me.
They haven't had time to dig really deep yet.'

'You're just being absurd!'

But she looked better and ate a forkful of sauté potatoes.
Then she asked:

'Will you be in Hong Kong going back to Singapore?'

'It's the only way out of here.'

'You'll have stopover time?'

'Probably.'

'It's just that I'd like to fix you an American dinner.
Would you like that?'

The fact that she was prepared to cook seemed to indicate a slow return to norm.

'Love it,' I said.

'It's all I can offer for the hospitality you've given me
here. I thought about you, too, last night.'

'Oh?'

'I know you're in some kind of trouble. I don't want to
be nosey, because I know you don't like that. All I'll say
is that I wouldn't leave Macao if I thought I could help.
Can I?'

'I doubt it.'

'You're not in any danger?'

'I wouldn't call it that. Just a complicated business thing.
The opposition is a bit active at the moment, that's all.
But it'll soon be sorted out.'

'I hope so. I'll worry until I hear from you in Hong
Kong. I'm in the phone book. You're certain there's nothing I can do?'

'Quite certain.'

She looked at me for some time, solemn.

'I don't think you ought to marry that Mrs Nival
whatever her name is.'

'I'll remember that next time I'm fighting out of a
corner.'

'What happened to her first husband?'

'She divorced him. Cruelty. The brute tried to pinch back her diamonds. A quarter of a million dollars' worth.'

Suddenly, surprising me, Amelia laughed.

One advantage of putting through a long-distance call from a central post office is that you can be pretty sure that even in a dictatorship your line out isn't bugged. But I still had quite a fight getting through to Singapore and when the number was finally buzzing I was suddenly sure that Ranya would be taking another of those long breaks during which she investigated the local restaurant business. I got her secretary, the one on probation, who didn't sound at all like a repentant sinner, anything she might be feeling coated away under a sophisticated drawl.

'Oh, Mr Harris, Mrs Nivalahannanda will be *so* glad you've rung. I'll put you right through.'

'Well,' said Ranya from her hand-polished teak desk. 'Nice of you to take time off from sixty-year-old Americans. If you hadn't rung I was going to catch a night plane to Hong Kong to be with you for breakfast tomorrow in your boarding-house. I'm rather curious about that boarding-house. It's the first time I've ever known you to leave the best hotel to go to one. Why?'

'I haven't time for explanations now, Ranya. I've just got minutes from a public box and after that we're cut off. I need your help.'

'Of course you do. You should have let me come with you.'

'Your help down there. I want you to fly to Kuala Lumpur first plane. Have Bahadur, my man there, waiting for you at the airport with a car. He'll take you to see Batim Salong. He knows where the house is.'

'Batim Salong is that prince, isn't he? Ever since my marriage to the cousin of one I've been allergic to princes.

They bring me out in a rash.'

'Ranya! I've lost my passport. I'm stuck in Macao until I get papers of some sort. Batim can get me a *laissez passer* or whatever they're called. Something like that. He can fix it at speed.'

'Why couldn't your man Bahadur do this?'

'Batim doesn't like Sikhs.'

'Just what am I being asked to pay for this pass of yours?'

'A small ration of your charm. Bahadur can keep the engine running.'

'There were a lot of things you didn't tell me about this business when you offered me a directorship. How did you lose your passport? Were you mugged?'

'Yes.'

'These days I only need one guess. Paul, you shouldn't be on your own up there. I'm coming up.'

'If you do you're sacked. I don't want anyone coming to Macao. Bahadur is to take what's necessary to Hong Kong and wait to hear from me in the Mandarin Hotel. You've got that? He's to do nothing at all about trying to get in touch with me over here.'

'All right.' Her tone changed. 'I don't like this. Have you written me about what's happening?'

'I don't have time at the moment for long letters. Have you found out what that American in Texas wants?'

'No. In spite of the fact that he uses trans-Pacific lines as if they were around the block. I'm beginning to dread the buzzer on my desk. He says his business can't wait. He won't believe that I don't know where you are. As vice-president I'm bound to know.'

'Who said you were vice-president? You?'

'In America they don't understand about directorships. Everyone who matters is a vice-president. It's something for you to think about in connection with me . . .'

There was a click and the line went dead. I had to go

over to the counter to get instructions on how to make a local call, usually I got waiters to do this for me. The phone buzzed for a long time up at the Villa Setubal and then a woman said :

'Yes.'

It was the same voice I'd had before, sounding as though she had a mouthful of rice. I identified myself and asked to speak to Teng Ching Wok. This was impossible since he was much worse than he had been at the time of my last inquiry. I got that, but not much else. I nearly told her to take time to swallow the rice, I could wait, but instead said :

'Please let him know I'm very sorry he's ill.'

'All right.'

As I came out of the booth Johnny Cass was going into another one. He spotted me.

'Hey, there. I won't be long. Hang on and I'll give you a ride wherever you want to go.'

An obliging young man. I waited, not more than three minutes. He came out again.

'Well, I guess I missed you this morning. I slept late. How was that great bed of yours?'

'Lonely. Also, the mattress travelled out here with the frame in the seventeenth century.'

'You didn't sleep?'

'Not all that well. It was probably my conscience. Yours ever trouble you?'

'Never.'

There was a walk in the sunshine to where he had parked the convertible. We got in and he lit a cigarette. I decided I was due a cigar and found the last of Long's Havanas, showing it great respect with a match. It was a nice public place for what I had to do, people passing all the time. 'I've been in touch with a man in Hong Kong who does odd jobs for me,' I said. 'A private investigator of sorts. He's good. Never made a mistake yet in anything he's undertaken. He says you aren't known in Kowloon refugee circles. Also, Father Pelham has never heard of you. Also, you'd only been in Hong Kong for a short time before you came here.'

Johnny Cass took the cigarette from his mouth and held it in one hand which he placed on the wheel to match his other hand which was also there. He stared up the street. I looked at a beautiful profile.

CHAPTER X

Staring into the middle distance is quite a good way of getting past an awkward moment or two. He really took his time, then said :

'Well, what do you make of it?'

I gave him full marks for pushing the next move over to me.

'My immediate reaction was that you're an employee of the CIA. But when I computer programmed this the answer was no.'

'Your computer's blown a circuit.'

'I don't think so. The CIA place their people carefully. They're never sent out into the world equipped with a background one cable can dissipate.'

'Even their rookies?'

'Is that what you claim to be?'

'Yes.'

'Then I'm not flattered. The last time the CIA were interested in me they used their number three man in South East Asia.'

'Your rating hasn't slipped much. You could say that Janey is their number four out here. I'm along for the ride.'

'Training course?'

'Yeh. And have I ballsed it up. I've been getting hell ever since I brought you back to the boarding-house. She says that set your antennae twitching.'

'How right she is. I reshuffled those data cards and put them in the slot again. You know what the machine came up with second time round?'

'I just couldn't guess.'

'You and Miss Daly are both honours graduates from the US section of that college near Magnitogorsk in the Soviet Urals. It wouldn't surprise me to learn that the two of you shared the special Lenin prize as the best students in your final year.'

He laughed but didn't look at me.

'I've never even heard of Magnitogorsk.'

'Maybe they took you there from Moscow in a sealed train?'

He went on staring at the road.

'Look, Mr Harris, are you saying I'm a Russian?'

'If you're not you're a period American. You just don't fit your age group. That could be because you're not the age group you look. These days they do a great job with hormone treatments.'

'I don't know what the hell you're talking about!'

'I think you do, Johnny. What I'm suggesting is that the year's practical you did in the States after graduation, and after being landed from a Soviet submarine in Oregon somewhere, was quite a while ago. You were a boy then but you're into your thirties now. And if you're a rookie I need my old Chinese nanny. Your bosses made a mistake in thinking they could use you on me for one last job before you got sent back to the States again on your sabbatical year. I may have a British background but I travel a lot, and I have a pretty good ear for idiom. Your American dates that intensive field course you did, putting it somewhere about 1958. Could just be 1960 but I don't think so late. Follow?'

'You're crazy, man, crazy!'

'Don't think you're updating yourself by throwing

"mans" at me. You got that stuff off a record, not from working recently in a Portland garage. How did you enjoy Portland back in the fifties?'

'Never been there in my life.'

'I'll tell you one place I'd bet big money you've never been and that's Dayton, Ohio.'

'Look, I don't know how good Portuguese psychiatrists are, but you need help.'

'Don't get me wrong, Johnny, I've nothing against the Russians. On the whole I welcome your presence out here. We need a counter balance to Peking with a big fist in reserve and where will we get this except from Moscow?'

'Mr Harris, you really shouldn't be sitting out in the sun without a hat.'

'Call me Paul. The age gap between us has closed considerably in the last ten minutes.'

He looked at me with a positively sweet smile.

'How old would you make Janey on *her* hormones?'

'Well, I don't want to seem rude, but I'd say she has been around for quite a while, too.'

He reached forward, switched on the engine, then said gently:

'I was going to take you somewhere. How about the local nerve clinic?'

'The old town will do nicely, thank you.'

We drove without any talk at all about Soviet strategy in the Far East, a subject which fascinates me, Johnny completely silent, though at the same time showing no personal stress of the kind that translates itself on to a steering-wheel, his driving careful and deeply considerate of pedestrians. He couldn't linger where I asked to be let out but as the convertible moved off I saw his eyes in the driving-mirror watching, so I just stood on the edge of a narrow pavement for a couple of minutes thinking about how laughably easy the free world is to penetrate. All you have to do is land from your submarine looking reasonably tidy and after that no one even asks to see all those beautifully forged proofs of identity you're carrying. In a country the size of the States any little idiosyncrasies in speech or manner can be put down, out on the Western Seaboard, to the fact that you're a refugee from New England. And if they started to round up all the people with little idiosyncrasies in Southern California a good third of the population would soon be under detention.

It was actually an American CIA man relaxing as my guest who told me all about the Magnitogorsk College where Johnny had studied for at least three years, living in the American village, using American plumbing, eating American food and drinking Pepsi-Cola except on Saturday nights when, at the carefully staged parties in a simulated rumpus room, he had to learn to drink bourbon on the rocks without wincing. Even in his sleep his new identity would have been fed into him electronically, but the big test was the practical, a year in the States without a specific assignment, his role simply to survive the time undetected. If he got through that all right he was ready for his first real part, probably something simple to start with like a US citizen in Chile on the run from an FBI narcotics charge.

The convertible had gone. I crossed to a shop and produced the paper with Wei Linfen's address, asking for directions. These put me in a narrow lane and the number I wanted seemed to be an antique dealer's with a sign in red Chinese characters on a black board. The man who ran it had a sage's beard which looked as though all the stronger hairs had been plucked out to make strings for one of those little portable lutes. His expressionless Oriental face showed real disappointment when he heard my Cantonese.

'I'm hunting for a little memento of this city.'

He continued to look sour.

'It doesn't have to be really old,' I said. 'A year or two would do.'

'Look around.'

'I have. What about your back room?'

'Nothing there.'

'Don't be ridiculous. You must do some real business?'

He stared at me.

'Where do you come from?'

'Singapore.'

'I might have known.'

We went through a curtain that wasn't beaded, looking as though it had been woven in Birmingham. There was plenty of dust behind it.

'What is it you're after?'

'A vase.'

He handed me one. It was pink.

'What do you call this?' I asked.

'*Famille rose,*' he said in French.

'I don't,' I said in Cantonese, and handed it back.

'That's a good piece!'

'It should be out front and you know it.'

I got another vase, Japanese Satsuma, embossed in gilt and quite horrible. I put that down, too, carefully. He was just longing to charge me for breakage.

'What about that then?'

It had a nice shape, imitation ox blood. An original would have been worth forty-five thousand dollars. I offered him three hundred escudos for it. His laughter was mirthless.

'Think you're an expert, eh?'

'No. But I do know there was a factory set up at King-teh-chen in the eighteen-nineties which turned out about twenty thousand of these copies for world museums until the demand ran out and they went bankrupt.'

'One thousand escudos,' he said.

'Three-fifty.'

'Seven hundred.'

'Four hundred, and that's my last offer.'

'You can have it for five-fifty.'

'All right. Put it in a wooden box.'

He took some time finding the box and from the way the vase and it fitted I decided that the two had been made for each other. The box was very aged-looking wood covered with faded Chinese characters almost certainly pre-dating the contents by four hundred years, these carefully applied recently in a bid to fool a Japanese buyer, Tokyo being the big market these days for bogus antiquities.

'A Miss Wei lives around here somewhere. How do I find her?'

He turned slowly, hostile again.

'If you mean one of those whores, up a stair at the side. I don't have anything to do with them.'

At his age I didn't think virtue earned much merit. I paid him, took my parcel and went out to look for the stairs. These were along an arched passage that seemed to lead at ground level into a labyrinth of courtyards. I climbed on noisy steps to a landing with four doors, none of them marked with name cards. I knocked on the first, waited, and knocked again. The girl who opened it had been asleep, needing her rest badly.

'Well?'

'I'm looking for Wei Linfen.'

Her eyes priced me. She might also have graduated from the waterfront.

'Over there. That door. But she's not in. Never is during the day. Some kind of job. I don't know much about her. Why do you want a cow like that?'

Miss Wei, daylighting on a second job, seemed to have put herself outside the sisterhood, re-classified back to amateur status.

'Does Wei Linfen have a pimp?'

'If I knew why should I tell you?'

I showed her a hundred and fifty escudos, pretty sure this was more than twice her fee for a short session.

'You'd better come in.'

It was her workroom and smelled like it. I didn't go very far in. A window had shutters closed against glare and not much air came through the slats. Two lamps were on, the bulbs masked under fluffy shades to give a light that would be kind to visitors' bodies. Blow-ups decorated the walls, one of Mao, but she was catholic in her political tastes and had another of Chiang Kai-shek.

She lit a cigarette and quite slowly worked her way into a description of a man which could have been made to fit somewhere around two hundred million Chinese until she got to the haircut which was skull short. Then she put up both hands and pushed her ears forward. For a quarter of a minute she might have been Ho Tai's younger sister.

I didn't need to hear any more. I put the money on a table. At the door I turned.

'I'll know if you tell anyone I've been asking questions, so don't.'

The old man was at the front of his shop.

'My girl wasn't in,' I said, shifting the parcel from one arm to the other. 'But I think I'm going to like this vase. I'll send all my friends to you.'

He glared.

The small café where I breakfasted had a telephone as well as what seemed to be only one man of all work on duty out front. He was a middle-aged Macanese who looked as though mixed racial genes had rubber stamped his failure rating a few weeks after conception. The place was almost empty, one couple at a table near the arch to the pavement who were no longer pretending in public that they had made anything of marriage. A Chinese read a newspaper in a corner over a glass of beer and a radio provided cover noise. My tip got quick service. I even had the dialling done, handed a burring receiver. That sound went on for so long I was about to hang up when a male voice said :

'Yes?'

It wasn't Ho Tai.

'Is that you, Teng?'

'Yes.'

'Up and about are you?'

There was no response. I didn't go on probing the state of his health.

'Listen, I've just clicked into place the last link in a chain that leads from me having my wallet stolen straight to you. Interested?'

He didn't seem to be.

'Are you still there?'

'Yes.'

'I'm sure the evidence I have would interest the police. Especially in a place where they're trying to build up tourism on a law and order ticket. After we've had our talk I'll decide whether I'm going to the police or not. But we're having that talk. Right away. So tell your man to open the gate when I ring.'

All I heard was Teng's breathing, which sounded like a dog sleeping. I hung up, got out my wallet and a Biro, wrote down the café's phone number and then extracted a couple of fifty escudo notes. The waiter was coming back from no tip for two coffees.

'I want you to keep this parcel for me. Will you be the one answering the phone here this afternoon?'

'Yes.'

'I should be ringing you back in about twenty minutes or at the most half an hour. If you don't get that call you're to ring the police. Tell them to go to the Villa Setubal expecting trouble. Break in if they have to. Understand?'

He nodded, showing no alarm at all.

'I'll double this money when I come back for my package. But if I phone in you forget about the police. Now get me a taxi.'

High walls made the narrow street past the Villa Setubal

look like a deep drain coming down from the hill. I paid off the hire and pulled the bell by wrought-iron, the gate swinging open before the car had turned. I went up steps to the hibiscus hedge and around this to the open garden beyond which had the tidy, not-for-use look of a display in a floral show. Up on the terrace the fountain wasn't working and the breeze I was expecting there hadn't arrived. It was hot, and though there was noise from the city the house preserved its own intense silence like a Japanese Imperial tomb.

Glare prevented me from seeing if there was anyone in the sitting-room and I was practically on top of a man in an arm-chair before I identified him. Teng Ching Wok was wearing a mauve dressing-gown loosely draped over bright blue pyjamas, a colour scheme that did nothing for him. He had one leg up on a stool like a gout victim, the rest of his body splayed out, both arms dangling.

'Nice of you to come,' he said heavily.

That was straight from the personality I had once known.

'Where's Ho Tai?'

'I should think with some bitch. But he's not in this house, if that's what's worrying you.'

'Who let me in?'

'I did. You see me recovering from the effort.'

'Where are your servants?'

'Cook's half-day. The maid seems to have taken one, too. I'm alone.'

'I'll just check on that.'

'By all means.'

At the door to the hall I said:

'When did Ho Tai leave?'

'About an hour ago.'

The hall was wide, tiled and rather dingy. It had four doors, one to a front bedroom that was obviously Teng's, also with sliding glass panels to the terrace, these open. I closed them and flipped the catch lock. Bedclothes were spilled out on the floor. The room next door was smaller with a single window of frosted glass. Along one whole wall was electronic equipment, short wave radio, tape recorder, a screen for the close-circuit television, and a portable walkie-talkie set which looked big enough to have considerable range. There was a bed, a chest and two chairs, plus clothes in a cupboard. Ho Tai lived close to his gadgets.

Another bedroom was sealed and musty smelling. There was a bathroom, but beyond this only a passage leading to a large kitchen not overly clean. I checked the windows here and locked a door leading to a court and, having secured my rear, went back to the living-room.

Teng was as I had left him but breathing better. He didn't turn his head as I dialled. The waiter must have been standing right by the instrument. I told him to hold that call to the police for an hour and a half.

'Covering yourself are you?' Teng said.

'Yes. Have you a gun?'

'Ho Tai took over my Colt. If he hadn't I might have shot him some time during the last few days.'

He was sounding very like the man I remembered. I went over to a chair which gave me a clear view of anyone coming up on to the terrace.

'K. K. Long blamed you for everything that has happened to me since I came to Macao. Are you passing that on to Ho Tai?'

'Much of it, yes.'

'You expect me to believe you?'

'No.'

'Teng, are you a prisoner in this place?'

'I'm the prisoner of my own body. I couldn't get down to that bloody gate by myself. So here I sit, looking at that view of hell's shithouse. I've got the same view from my bed.'

'Here you sat directing operations against me with OSL.'

I recognized that sudden grin.

'So I did. It was a real interest for me. Something to get my teeth into again. After years of keeping the books for petty trading.'

'What kind of trading?'

'Refugees into Hong Kong. I bought a junk with all the portable assets I got out of Malaysia. It turned out to be a good investment.'

'Your fares a hundred and fifty dollars against two dollars on the ferry?'

'A little less. Competition has been hotting up recently. The traffic is lighter, too.'

'As the result of another outlet for male refugees?'

He hoisted his other leg on to the stool, grunting. I could see how swollen his ankles were.

'I wonder who has been talking to you, Paul. Long?'

'No.'

'Are you up on behalf of Inspector Kang as well as yourself?'

'Just myself. Did you carry heroin on your junk?'

'Junks. I have three now. Or had. I sold out when I became a Long operative. He likes his people snow white.'

'What about the heroin?'

He nodded.

'That, too.'

'It's a pretty dirty business for a man who lives within the Marxist ethic.'

'Who used to live within the Marxist ethic. Ethics are for the successful. A man who finds himself in my position just survives . . . or not. And taking the long view what's so dirty about the heroin trade? The sooner the West is debauched the better for the rest of us. We're only serving you back what you served us a century ago. Remember those opium wars? So don't sit there looking holy. When your grandfather went to Shanghai Chinese customs were run by Britons to line British pockets.'

'My grandfather was an importer-exporter.'

'That's a beautiful cover-all. I'm sure Harris and Company's trading accounts for 1890 would make interesting reading these days. Have you still got them locked away somewhere?'

'No.'

'Probably burned when the old man decided to emigrate south and turn over a new leaf. How abut pouring me a large brandy?'

'I thought you weren't drinking?'

'That was when I still believed I had a future.'

'You don't now?'

'No.'

'When was the moment of truth?'

'A few days ago. Ho Tai came into my room and ripped out the phone by my bed. He left the one in here because he didn't think I'd ever be able to get as far as this again. I knew then I was redundant. Long had decided to use Ho Tai as his local man.'

'Have you an idea what they mean to do with you?'

'Not really. But KKL is tidy minded. He doesn't leave loose ends lying about. My hope is that it won't be painful. I've always been a coward about pain. How about that drink?'

I got up and went over to the side table with bottles, pouring a brandy, then a whisky.

'Anything in it?' I asked.

'No, straight. My easy flow of confession has thrown you somewhat, hasn't it?'

'Yes.'

'Well, you see you came at exactly the right time. I was feeling lonely. And you're part of my beautiful past.'

'Catching up with you.'

I gave him his glass.

'That, too,' he agreed, and took a big gulp.

I sat down with the weird feeling of being comfortable again with this monster. He wasn't a coward. No future had put him back inside himself.

'You're much more mobile than Ho Tai realizes,' I said. 'How about getting out of here?'

'Where to?'

'You must have relatives?'

'I have one brother who emigrated to Sandakan from Malaysia to become an eminently respectable dealer in jungle hardwoods. When I had to leave home fast under a cloud we lost touch.'

'A Chinese family will always take in one of its members, whatever his past. Sandakan might be a good place for you. Out of the main stream. Your enemies will forget you're still alive.'

Teng smiled.

'Nice thought. How would I get there?'

'As an ex-junk owner that ought to be easy to fix.'

'Yes. I saw one of them at anchor this morning. All its backside decoration is bright red. We believed that the more conspicuous you are the less likelihood of arousing suspicion. It's worked very well. We've always been able to get a bribe to the right search officer in time to blunt his intensive hunt for access to the big compartment in our false bottom.'

I stood, took binoculars from a cabinet and went out on to the terrace. There were at least forty of the larger junks at anchor out in the deeper water, but I picked out one with bright red paint.

'See her?' Teng called out.

'I think so.'

'You ought to be able to make out her name . . . *Golden Morning Pavilion*. Big characters. But I'd forgotten, you don't read Chinese.'

I came back into the room and stood looking down at him. Both his feet were on the floor as though he was testing them out. If this was painful his face wasn't putting out any signals, he seemed only interested in me.

'Tell me if I'm imagining things, Paul, but are you considering offering me a helping hand?'

'Yes.'

'Bones of my ancestors! Isn't that carrying humanity to absurd lengths?'

'It would be if it was my only reason. But I want out of Macao, too. And by a back door.'

'Ah, of course. You have no passport. And we would be dropping you off from *Morning Pavilion* in Hong Kong?'

'Yes.'

'This is a very wild idea,' Teng said.

'They can be made to work. How long is Ho Tai likely to be away?'

'At least some hours. When he goes to his woman he takes his time. And the fact that he's got rid of the maid suggests that he may plan to be away all night. He's done that before. Leaving me alone contributes to the disintegration of my morale. I made a great mistake when I brought that man from Malaysia, I ought to have offered him up as a sacrifice to your Superintendent Kang down in Singapore. I was stupid enough to imagine that as well as being my colleague he was a friend. There are no such things.'

'I'm acting like a friend.'

'You are acting like a man wanting out of Macao fast in order to put yourself one up on K. K. Long. I wonder if Che Fa would do it?'

'The skipper of your junk?'

'Yes. Unfortunately there has been some bad feeling between us. As head man of my little fleet he didn't think his cut of the price when I sold up was good enough. I gave him five per cent, quite adequate.'

'We could pay him a fat fee for the job,' I said.

'So we could.'

'Ho Tai hasn't got hold of your money?'

'Not yet. Fortunately I had the sense to make that rather difficult for him. With a numbered account in that country whose Alps will endure long after the rest of the world has crumbled. The number is in my head, nowhere else. I might reveal it under hypnosis or drugs, I suppose. But so far that hasn't been tried.'

'So if you got to Sandakan you wouldn't be dependent on your brother?'

'Fortunately not. As one of our poets put it, roughly : "To eat the rice of relations, ah, sad heart." '

He was sitting back now in the chair looking as though the brandy had really relaxed him.

'You know, Paul, I'm becoming curious about things again. It must be a sign of hope returning. Do you mean to tie up with Long?'

'That's my business.'

'Of course. I can see your position. You've always been handicapped by a curiously sensitive conscience, haven't you? Which means that now you have some moral scruples to chloroform before you say yes. You'd also like to accept from a position of some strength, which means not being cooped up here in Macao when you do it. I suggested to Long that he was making a mistake in subjecting you to the claustrophobia of this place. God knows I've had experience of that feeling for long enough. But, of course, the great man didn't listen to me. He regards advice as an impertinence. At one time I was starting to adopt that attitude myself. The real danger with power is not that it corrupts but that it isolates. You think you're immune in your remoteness and suddenly you trip over a very small wire placed as a trap. Just as I did.'

'We'll have time for the Teng Ching Wok life story on board that junk. Right now I want to know how I get in touch with Che Fa.'

'It should be quite simple. *Golden Morning Pavilion* is his flagship and he'll certainly be on her. I'll give you a note. You can get it out to him by a water boat woman. If Che agrees to our proposition he raises and lowers his foresail. I'll offer him two thousand dollars for our passages, that ought to be enough. You can give me your cheque for one thousand when we're on board. You wait down on the waterfront for the signal and if it is yes you come back to collect me.'

'What if I come back to find that Ho Tai has returned to nurse you?'

'In that case you deal with the man. Some time about midnight. He's a heavy sleeper and he'll be snoring after his woman. Should be no problem at all to an active man like you.'

'Aren't you forgetting one thing? How do I get in here?'

'With my key.'

'I saw no lock.'

'You turn down one of the metal flowers, then slide in a piece of steel which breaks the circuit.'

'Your servants have these keys?'

'Certainly not. They are inspected each morning. There are only two. I have one. Ho Tai has the other.'

'Where do you keep yours?'

'In a cufflinks box in the top right hand drawer of my chest.'

I went out and over to Teng's bedroom. I found the cufflinks box, with cufflinks, but no key. I looked in the other drawers, then went back to the living-room.

'Ho Tai has the second key. He probably decided to take custody of it about the time he yanked out your phone.'

Teng finished his brandy. He still wasn't using that stool for his legs.

'I see. It looks as though I'll have to deal with Ho Tai

myself. And let you in.'

'Think you could?'

'With the prospect of a future again, yes. There are still kitchen knives. You can bring me one before you leave. Or would it trouble you to be party to murder?'

'Not in this case.'

He smiled.

'I didn't think it would.'

'It would still be better if you came with me now, Teng.'

He shook his head.

'I'm not exposing myself to Macao in daylight. There are others here who would be interested to know that I was leaving and try to prevent it. Also, in my state, transhipping me from a taxi to a sampan is going to take time and might attract attention. At night we could manage it all right. Also, if Che Fa says no you would have no alternative but to bring me back here. In these circumstances I wouldn't enjoy being met by Ho Tai. Get me paper and a pen. That desk.'

The sampan taking a note to the *Golden Morning Pavilion* seemed to be scarcely moving, its stern oar barely tickling the water. I walked up and down the sea side of the Praya trying to look like a tourist fascinated by the sights and sounds of a Far Eastern anchorage. The daily ferry from Hong Kong arrived at least an hour behind schedule and that gave me something else to stare at.

There were hints of sunset in the sky, streaky colours a prologue to the big display. I carried on to the park and sat on a bench beyond the statue which turned out not to be an effigy of Dr Salazar, but someone called Ferreira do Amaral. The man up there had the look of a colonial governor who had been through a lot of trouble with his Chinese neighbours, a worried bronze face.

The rower had now reached the *Golden Morning Pavilion* and gone around to her offside. She was a big junk, broad beamed to allow for her false bottom, a sea-going version of one of those houseboats more or less permanently anchored behind Hong Kong island to form a floating town. There was a fair chance that she was powered by a couple of Harris diesels. I don't know who buys my engines from my northern agencies and it can be just a little disturbing to consider the uses to which one of your products may have been put. It is the kind of moral dilemma which faces many businessmen these days, but at least I don't sell machine-guns. And if you are going to survive in the Orient against competition pieces of your conscience have to be kept in deep freeze. The most I'll say for myself is that I take the pieces out from time to time to have a look at them before popping them back into store again.

The sampan reappeared after long enough for the rower to have enjoyed a cup of tea and bean cakes on board. Ten minutes later, and under a sky gone flamboyant, the *Golden Morning Pavilion* hoisted a sail, but the wrong one, on her mainmast. She travelled on an offshore breeze without engines, drifting slowly towards my end of the Praya. The anchor went down again and the mainsail was dropped, the junk in total isolation on a brightness from reflecting water. For perhaps twenty minutes there was no activity at all but finally a man came out from her high stern poop and walked slowly along the well deck towards the shorter foremast, pottering around at the foot of this. The small ribbed sail came creaking up, a deep maroon signal flag triumphing over the now fading pyrotechnics from the sky.

It was dark by the time a taxi set me down at the Villa Setubal; I had detoured to leave my vase at the Castello Blanco and to buy the longest handled flashlight I could find. The only contact I had in Macao who could have produced a gun at short notice was Alvares and

I had a feeling that his professional ethics might have complicated the deal. A long-handled flash which swells out
at the bulb end isn't a bad weapon for close range work.

I paid the driver, then turned towards the stone arch.
With no lights behind it the gate was in deep shadow. Suddenly a lean mongrel dog came running out from the villa's
garden to yap first at me, then the turning taxi. I stood
still until the car was moving down the hill and the dog,
a coward, had decided to follow it. My flash showed the
grille wide back, held by a large rock. The invitation just
to walk in didn't appeal to me very much.

When I shoved the stop out of the way with my foot the
barred gate felt completely slack under my hand, as
though the circuit powering the open-shut mechanism had
been switched off. I let it go and it shut all right but there
was no click from an electric lock, and it swung back again
under the touch of my hand.

I went up the path using light very sparingly and cutting
it out altogether at the hibiscus hedge. There was no glow
from the house. On the terrace I could just see that the
sliding glass wall of the living-room was open on to blackness. I made checking up on the *Golden Morning Pavilion*'s
position an excuse for not at once going inside, and
located the junk all right, one red riding light positioned
by itself a good quarter of a mile from a nebula of these.

Half a dozen table lamps confirmed what my torch had
already suggested, the living-room was empty. Teng's
brandy glass was still on the table and there was no hint
of anything disturbed. I went to the front bedroom which
was much tidier than when I had last seen it, the bed made,
its cover drawn tight. There was no one in the operations
centre, the bathroom or the guestroom with an unused
smell. In the kitchen I found the back door still locked
and nothing to indicate that anyone had been there recently.

Ho Tai's work bench had a panel of switches, none

M

of them marked. I had activated the short-wave radio and a tape recorder before I got any reaction from the scanner screen, a humming blackness flecked with white dots. Other switches seemed to be for garden lighting and, though I couldn't see this, I had illumined the pool and started up the terrace fountain before the screen produced a bright picture of the gate area, together with sound, for I heard a car going down the road beyond. The gate circuit control was set on a flat surface, like a mini-gear lever, now at 'off'. I pushed it to 'on', then pressed a button set alongside, watching the screen. The grille swung open, held for seconds, then swung back again. I was locked into this mini estate, and I hoped without company.

The tape recorder was still whirring. I said 'good evening' to myself, then pushed the play-back key. There was no message. I set the tapes moving again, crossed the hall to the living-room, and standing just inside the door commented that it was a fine night. Back in operations I found that my weather item had been duly recorded. I switched off and then went to pour myself the whisky I needed, taking the glass out to the terrace.

The Villa Setubal was all lit up for a party, the fountain spraying coloured jets, the pool bright from underwater bulbs as well as the Japanese lanterns edging it, while the path to the gate was a white, twisting ribbon under silhouetted trees. Over all this shine I could still make out the *Golden Morning Pavilion*'s one red eye. It seemed to move. I didn't believe that and sipped whisky. Then I had to go in for Teng's binoculars.

These had good magnification. The junk's shape was a bit muzzed by darkness but I could make out her well deck clearly enough and there was no doubt that both her sails were up, though she was obviously still under power, and with throttles open. She was travelling fast enough for me to have to keep moving the glasses. A door in the poop opened, a splash of white, and against this were figures, men who might be standing at a rail looking up towards a hill on which a villa glowed like a radio beacon.

One of those figures was almost certainly Teng Ching Wok. The bastard had simply used me to make his arrangements, his invalidism an act. He had seen that sunset signal from where I stood now, and had then ordered a taxi. Swollen ankles or not he had got down that path by himself. It was Sandakan first stop, if that was where his brother really lived, though it could be anywhere, the Philippines, Celebes, Halmahera.

A buzzer sounded in the house. I crossed the living-room and hall, switching on the screen. A man in a grey suit and carrying a briefcase was standing beyond the grille. It was K. K. Long.

CHAPTER XI

I used the switch to open the gate, flicked on the tape recorder as I passed it, then went back to the terrace, standing to look down at the bright path. Long came up it with a bouncing agility which was a wonderful ad for that Chinese keep-fit dance routine. Half-way on the last flight he glanced up. I was well illumined. He almost missed his step, did a gull flutter for balance, then stopped.

'Paul! What on earth are you doing here?'

He finished the climb. His breathing wasn't fast.

'Where's Teng?'

I didn't tell him where I thought Teng was. We had a short session of wondering whatever could have happened and then went into the sitting-room where Long put his case on a glass-topped table exactly like a man taking temporary possession of a fifty-dollar-a-day hotel suite. He stared at the used brandy glass as though outraged by this reminder of a previous occupant, looking as though he wanted to ring room service to have the offending object removed.

'You say you found the gate open? No signs of violence anywhere?'

'Everything is perfectly tidy.'

'Extraordinary situation.'

'Yes, isn't it? When did you arrive in Macao?'

'Less than an hour ago.'

'From the *Hui Yang*?'

He nodded, then sat down. Mr Pu could make jokes about having to look up to people, but Mr Long just hated doing it.

'Sit down, Paul, sit down.'

I took the chair opposite. He reached forward to unlock the briefcase with a key from his personal ring. I said:

'I hope you've got my passport in there?'

He looked up. He might have been a psychiatrist who is never even momentarily disturbed by anything a patient may say. His voice was gentle.

'How am I supposed to react to that?'

'By handing it over.'

'What happened to your passport?'

'I was mugged and it was stolen. By Ho Tai.'

'Ho Tai . . .?'

'Teng's muscle man. You will remember him from your last visit.'

'Oh, yes. And just how does this incident lead to me?'

'An hour or so after it happened I heard your helicopter take off.'

'You think I had been waiting for the document to arrive?'

'Yes.'

His surprise wasn't a bad act. He tended to type himself somewhat, keeping to a limited range of performances, and I suspected that there was a lot of ham in Mr Pu at Ascot. But that wouldn't matter since Ascot is all ham anyway.

'Let me get this straight, Paul. You think I got hold of your passport in order to keep you marooned here in Macao?'

'Of course. But don't think I hold it against you. In your shoes I might have done the same thing.'

'Really?'

He gave me a tight smile.

'If you don't have the thing,' I said, 'how could you be sure I was still here?'

'I rang Alvares this morning. He said you were.'

'Your new local agent?'

'*Our* new local agent. Don't you approve?'

'I suppose every big corporation needs at least one bent lawyer. Are you planning to give Teng a golden handshake?'

'No.'

I hadn't expected he would but I did feel he might have suggested we phone the local hospital to find out whether our host had been admitted for emergency treatment. He began to fish about inside the briefcase, pulling out two quarto-sized folios in plastic covers, one red, the other green. He pushed these over the table towards me. I saw characters stamped in gold.

'Perhaps you would like to start reading, Paul?'

'That seems to be in Chinese.'

'Oh, sorry. It's the other copy. They are both identical in so far as the limited number of characters on one of our typewriters permits an exact copy. But the Chinese version is only for reference. You sign the English.'

'What about witnesses?'

'They'll sign later. And please don't suggest that this is illegal.'

I got the controlled smile again. He was being determinedly amiable to erase all memories of how our last contact had ended.

'Will you take me to Hong Kong on the *Hui Yang* when we've cleared up our business?'

'I'm sorry, but I can't do that. The *Hui Yang* is now *en route* for Formosa. I'll be travelling on tonight's ferry to Hong Kong. It would be better if you waited until tomorrow. Also, I'm keeping my ship very clear of British waters just at the moment.'

'Your yacht was searched?'

'Oh, yes. Water police. Two British officers and about ten Chinese. I'm told they were on board for two hours. Very polite, but looking everywhere. For drugs, they said. I have registered a strong official protest from Taiwan.'

'Which is where you are supposed to be now?'

'Yes.'

'You'll travel tonight as Mr Pu?'

He nodded. However he might travel it wasn't Mr Pu in Teng's sitting-room.

'Incidentally,' he said, 'convenient as it is for me to have found you waiting, it wasn't what I was expecting. Why did you come to see Teng?'

'I've been ringing him up and getting a girl who seemed pretty stupid. I thought if I stood at the grille and looked like making a scene out there in the street they might let me in. Even a recluse worries about what the neighbours may think.'

'You haven't answered my question. Why did you want to see Teng?'

'To interrogate him.'

'What about?'

'Mostly you.'

He didn't smile.

'Why not put any questions you have about me to me?'

'Thank you, I will. Question one, are you as concerned

about security as you ought to be?'

'Security?'

'Yes. I must say I see big flaws in some of your arrangements. I might even call them areas of serious risk. As in the recruitment of your crews. Obviously you have the Greeks beaten to a stop here, but it could still become a very exposed flank of our operations.'

It was a matter of some seconds before he said:

'I'm afraid I'm not following you at all?'

'I'm talking about your intake of Macao refugees.'

Again the pause, then his voice, very gentle:

'Please go on.'

'It's the possibility of this thing being made public which worries me. And it's obvious that the danger increases as your fleets grow bigger. We could wake up one morning to find ourselves facing an investigating commission from the United Nations. Their findings just might result in some kind of sanctions against KKL ships, and that would mean everything you've set up simply blasted by publicity. You'd be set in pillory by the liberal Press all over the world, with any amount of muck coming at you.'

He was the cement statue again, this time seated. His lips scarcely moved when he spoke.

'You've been busy. Where did you get this information?'

'Some of it by observation. A batch of new recruits were carried during my voyage on the *Hui Yang*. I saw them loaded when I was supposed to be asleep. To prevent me seeing them unloaded near Taiwan, and I suspect ferried over to your training ship, I was drugged.'

'Idiots!'

'Oh, I wouldn't blame your staff too much. They had to deal with me at short notice and hadn't been properly briefed. You were watching horses.'

'Where else did you hear about this?'

'From a Macao whore who used to be on the boats. She told me that if she'd been a man she'd have gone to your ships. You can imagine I was very interested. It seems that nearly all the water people know about the KKL recruitments. And even though they keep to themselves and don't talk to the police, what happened to me could happen to any visitor to this town. I'd say that this is already a great big hole in security. Do you think you can plug it?'

'Yes.'

'I certainly hope so. Tell me, would I be expected to use your trained refugees in the Hok Lin fleet?'

'It would be economic to do so. And if you don't it will be almost impossible to find the crews you'll need for the expansion I've outlined.'

'This will be my first experience of running prison ships.'

For a moment it looked like an explosion. His face seemed to swell up around the still tight, but pulsing crater of his mouth, like a geyser about to come into action. Then the eruption was cancelled. Tactics took over. In a moment he was sounding a bit like Counsel who allows himself to come near to tears during his last address to the jury.

'My crews are not slaves, Paul. They are grateful men. I give them security, something they have never known. What future would they have without me?'

'Not much, I grant you. And don't worry, I see perfectly well what an advantage this gives us. We're practically back to the industrial revolution. Except that the Victorian ironmasters had to go to the trouble of encouraging the breeding of the mass cheap labour they needed. We have an endless flow directed straight at us.'

He sat back in his chair, not exactly relaxed, but no longer rigid.

'I have a feeling that some strange ethic of yours is offended,' he suggested. 'Am I right?'

'Well, I admit I had a little difficulty at first in coming to terms with the idea. It could be Presbyterian ancestry, the importance of the individual soul and all that. Grandfather got well away from his heritage here, but I've found myself drifting back towards it at times.'

'The rich man's son turned idealist?'

I smiled at him.

'That would be too much to claim. Just little spurts of conscience salving, that's all. Nothing that need worry us.'

'What sort of conscience salving?'

'Once I was active in a bid to suppress the indentured labour system that used to operate in these parts. I did a bit of snooping for the people investigating it. Wasn't that in my dossier?'

'No.'

'Well, it was years ago. But I did have the feeling then, and still do, that indentured labour is just a form of slavery. Though, of course, slavery with a term. The men signed on for a time and were free to go home at the end of it. Do your refugees ever get free to go home?'

Again there was that hint of the geyser, but the twitching lips quietened.

'My people are very happy indeed not to be living in a cardboard shanty up a Macao creek. Or in a Hong Kong slum.'

'Of course. You're really a philanthropist?'

'Don't try to be funny, Paul! I'm a man who makes use of conditions I find around me. I didn't create them. And I'm doing something to help many poor wretches no one else bothers with. You can say this is to the profit of KKL, all right, I admit it. But let me point out this, there is very little difference between my use of these former refugees and Japanese industrial paternalism. And as you know perfectly well the East is accustomed to paternalism. It suits us. I offer security in return for service.'

'Bound service.'

'Aren't Japanese workers bound to their companies?'

'They can leave if they want to. Admittedly no one else in Japan would take them on after such a breach of loyalty, but still the choice is there. And they are living in communities, normal family lives. Do your men live normal family lives?'

'What sailors do?'

'I see. This system doesn't apply to your office staff?'

'Of course not. They are mostly married men, with homes in Taiwan.'

'No homes in Taiwan for your sailors?'

'It's not so simple. I am considering a retirement island off Borneo.'

'What about women before they retire?'

'That too may become possible.'

'As an alternative to sex movies?'

Controlling anger had brought out little beads on Long Kin's forehead.

'It's very hot in here, Paul. Do you think you could shut the doors and put on the air-conditioning?'

'By all means.'

I got up and slid the glass panels along their runners, then went over to find the conditioner switch. It was an oldish machine and produced a hum with a rattle at intervals, like a fan heater with a loose connection. As I came back across the room I asked:

'Are you ready for question two?'

'Certainly.'

'Who finances KKL?'

'What do you mean? My business is self financing!'

'I don't believe it.'

I stood looking down at him. He hated that. His eyes were small.

'You've had backers from the very beginning,' I said. 'That rags to riches story you serve the Press isn't good enough for me. Also, its balls for our time. You can make a million or two from some new gimmick, but the really big money comes from money. The world's richest men had rich fathers. You've had a rich uncle.'

'And who is my rich uncle?'

'Peking.'

The noise he made may have been intended to be a laugh, but it didn't come out quite like that.

'Another whore told you this? Or the same one?'

'Just deduction. Aided by the feeling that I got on board the *Hui Yang* that the whole ship was a bit Peking orientated.'

'Why should China give me money?'

'To be their front man. The same blueprint you were going to use with me and Hok Lin.'

'I asked you . . . why should China use *me*?'

'You're ideal for their purpose. They need foreign exchange on a long-term basis. A lot of it. They haven't much to sell so they decided to become the world's carriers. Gambling a sizeable chunk of their gold reserves on you. That's how you've been able to move through the shipping business like a department store owner's son working his way up from the basement. A miraculous triumph of genius with a big hand pushing it. When you switched from tramps to the really big bottoms I thought your financing would have to come out in the open. But it didn't. Not a peep about it in Hong Kong or London or New York. You were just the new Chinese wonder boy who had suddenly leaped into the middle of the shipping stage wearing a gold mask. And you played the mystery man as well as Howard Hughes. Maybe better. I don't think Hughes has a Mr Pu available for recreation.'

Long Kin took out his gold case. It pleased me to see that his hand was shaking slightly both over the selection of a cigarette and in his use of a gold lighter.

'I'd be interested to know why you think China couldn't build up her own merchant fleet without outside help?'

'She could do, but only up to a point. That Peking

flag seen everywhere on the world seas might have built up considerable customer resistance. There's still a lot of prejudice about in spite of those newly opened doors. And a massive Chinese fleet might even have resulted in a commercial yellow peril flap. Also, even if Western capitalists were quite happy about having their goods carried cheaply in Chinese bottoms Russia wouldn't have liked this development at all. She might have switched her huge marine output from cruisers to trading ships for the kind of price war we've been contemplating in the Indian Ocean. And it wouldn't be so easy to win against them. No shareholders in that company dictating policy to management. These are the reasons why China needed you, Kin, staunch supporter of free enterprise as you are and so remote from any taint of Marxism in that island base of yours.'

I had to pause for breath like a tenor who has stretched himself on a high note. It seemed to me that Long was inhaling at a faster rate than is usually necessary when you're sitting in a chair.

'You have the *Hui Yang* just in case the worst should happen and Taiwan go back to the motherland. But even in your refugee role you'd get applause, clever Chinese tycoon nips out from under Peking's spreading net. You could even move headquarters to Macao, splendid gesture that, a man prepared to sit on the fringe of enemy territory thumbing his nose at the big threat. I pumped Alvares about whether you had any plans to turn this place into a free port, but it looks as though you haven't got around to these yet. But I'd say it was an idea to keep in mind.'

'You are full of ideas, Paul. It might be nearer it to call them fantasies. But let us suppose this marvellous fiction of yours even had an element of truth in it . . . how would that affect your reaction to our joint project?'

'It wouldn't affect it at all,' I said, turning away. 'I'm going to have a whisky. You'd like something?'

'A gin and tonic.'

At the drinks table I said:

'There's no ice here. Shall I get some from the kitchen?'

'Don't bother. Paul, you're a curious mix, sensitive about my refugee crews but apparently not troubled by your idea that in working for me you'd also be working for Peking. Am I right here?'

'Not quite, no.'

He was looking for something in his briefcase.

'Oh?' He didn't turn his head. 'So you don't like the idea of that, either?'

'I don't like the idea of having anything to do with your bloody enterprises. So you know what you can do with that contract.'

The Colt in his hand was a shock. I was beyond effective range from a man in an arm-chair, but he fired anyway. That first bullet shattered the whisky decanter. The second followed my roll across the floor towards shelter behind a padded sofa. A third smacked into the sofa. I heard the hiss from a punctured cushion. I knew he was coming over to put a bullet down into my back. It wasn't easy to wait until he was near enough to give me a chance in a dash for a glass door.

I heard one of these rumble on its runners. There was a sound like a champagne cork coming out, then a shout:

'No!'

A silenced gun fired again. Something bumped the sofa, pushing it back against me. I stayed on all fours until a voice said in Cantonese:

'You can get up now.'

I knew the voice, not the face. The girl looking down at me was wearing blue denims but it was a good few seconds before I recognized Miss Wei Linfen without her make-up.

It isn't too easy to rise with dignity from the prescribed position for Mohammedan prayer. I used the back of the sofa. Long Kin was lying along the front of it, both his arms almost neatly tucked in against his body. He was certainly dead. A high velocity bullet had split his skull. That part wasn't at all neat.

I looked towards the glass screens. Jane Daly and Johnny Cass were standing side by side just inside a three-foot opening in these. Jane was wearing an attractive pale blue two-piece trouser suit and had her hair tucked away inside a matching headscarf, but Johnny and she weren't playing sartorial twins this evening, his outfit practical for night work, black shirt, black trousers. In his right hand was the Luger. It is an ugly gun at any time but fitted with a silencer it becomes positively hideous, suggesting a small cannon. He had it pointed towards the floor now, but his stare directed straight at me was iced.

Miss Wei used the first English I had heard from her. 'You sit down.'

I wasn't sure whether this was a suggestion or an order. 'That might be a good idea,' I said.

My muscles seemed to have stiffened up, as though from a monster injection, and though I was perfectly aware of what was happening I felt at one remove from it, while at the same time able to tab this as shock reaction. I walked stiffly around the end of the sofa, avoiding blood and brains from that shattered head.

'You want whisky?' It was Wei Linfen again.

'Thanks.'

She used Russian. I don't speak any but I know what it sounds like. Johnny gave the gun to Jane, then walked across to the drinks table. From there he said :

'The whisky took a bullet.'

'Brandy will do,' I told him.

Blood had reached an Indian rug, this blotting it up, the contest with other dyes producing a tea-coloured, growing stain. Wei Linfen came over to take what had been Long's seat, directly opposite mine. There appeared to be only one gun in the party. Johnny was the killer imported specially for this assignment when it looked 'like things were moving towards a climax. As a professional he was probably a bit troubled about having had to use two bullets on target. He came over with my drink, which was Portuguese fire water, but the antidote to muscle seizure. Miss Wei looked up from inspecting the briefcase to say in Cantonese:

'Weren't you expecting him to be carrying a gun?'

'No.'

'Why not?'

'Same reason you're not carrying one. The officer commanding gives the order to fire, he doesn't do the shooting himself. I thought Long would hire an assassin to deal with me if I became a nuisance. And I'm certain he didn't bring that gun from his ship. I think he got it from Ho Tai. Which means they met this afternoon some time.'

'They did,' Wei Linfen said. 'Long came on the ferry. Ho Tai was waiting for him with the Cadillac. The ferry was late.'

'I know.'

'Did he tell you he'd come on his yacht?'

'Yes.'

'It isn't anywhere in this area.'

She seemed quite certain of that, and her information on the matter was likely to be highly accurate.

'Long and Ho Tai came here together from the ferry?'

She nodded.

'And then?' I asked.

'They carried Teng down to the car. He is now on the way to Canton for special treatment at a kidney clinic there. Or that's what I was told.'

'By that time you were back on duty here?'

'Yes.'

'I began to suspect you were the maid in this house when I discovered your connection with Ho Tai. How did you get the job? By sleeping with him?'

She might not have heard, reaching out for the Chinese

version of my unsigned agreement with K. K. Long.

'Was Teng drugged when they took him away?'

'Very much so. It was like moving a dead elephant. It took them half an hour to the gate. I had to help sometimes.'

'How can you be sure that Cadillac left Macao?'

'Because it was seen going through the gate. There was no hold-up on the other side. Everything had been arranged. Your friend had come to the end of his usefulness here in Macao.'

Teng Ching Wok had earned exactly what he was getting, but I still didn't like to think about him being driven, unconscious, towards the thing I was certain he feared most. He would get that treatment for his kidneys and afterwards probably be assigned a room somewhere to rot out what was left of his life. I wondered who would turn up as his proxy with the number for that Swiss account.

Wei Linfen was reading a Chinese text from back to front, her eyes going up and down its pages, not that I could see her eyes, just the movement of her head. She had reason to be pleased with this evidence in her hands, the timing putting it there good. Both Jane and Johnny had left the room. I sipped my brandy, the anaesthetic of shock no longer operative. I didn't much like my own position in all this. I had been the catalyst and catalysts are often just disposed of when they have completed their function.

Without her make-up Miss Wei Linfen might have come straight from a ribbed yak skin tent out on the Gobi Desert. It wouldn't be any long shot to guess that she had gone to school in Ulan Bator, capital of the USSR's important buffer ally, and that she had grown up speaking Ural-Altaic. I could just see her, too, winning the year's brightest student scholarship to Moscow University. Certainly those tiny eyes were a dead give away of Mongolian racial origins, slits from half a million years of squinting against sandstorms, but this wouldn't really be a risk factor to her later work in China as a Soviet agent. The country has a hundred ethnic groups, including many Southern Mongolians.

As I saw the overall picture Miss Wei had been ordered to drop her work in China and slip into Macao, assigned to cover Teng's activities, this probably immediately after his new connection with KKL had been discovered. Teng was the natural lead to Long himself, and the Russians were even more interested in the tycoon than I had been, their investigation requiring someone with much experience and high espionage rank.

It was obvious that Wei Linfen held this, very much senior to Jane Daly and Johnny. She didn't flaunt authority at all, just wore it, while at the same time was clearly prepared to do most of the dirty work herself, which is real leadership. That scene in the Algarve Hotel in my absence had been staged so that I wouldn't be allowed back in when I returned, forced to move to accommodation in which I would be highly accessible. Her visit to my room at the Castello Blanco was to serve me the facts about refugee recruitment because she was pretty certain that if I was issued with this ammunition I just wouldn't be able to resist using it during my negotiations with Long, if only to show what a bright boy I was. And she had been absolutely right here, my big turn producing precisely the crisis situation she had hoped for.

It would have been ungenerous not to give Miss Wei Alpha plus for planning, at the same time if she was an honest woman she would have to admit that she'd had a real gambler's run of good luck. Had I signed with Long on board his yacht, and just returned to Macao to pick up my suitcases, her whole operation against KKL would have failed, at least for this phase. Further, Long would have been back again behind that remarkable security curtain of his and not easy to get at. I doubted that she

N

even guessed about the existence of Mr Pu, and but for me she could have gone on as maid at the Villa Setubal for years, putting in the kind of reports to headquarters that would have done her no good at all. I hoped that she was capable of gratitude, but looking at that utility face across a table gave me the feeling that probably her only virtue was a passion for tidiness. This could so easily mean that when they had got all they wanted from me I would just be swept away.

Long had certainly been swept away. His assassination had been scheduled for when he was with me and carrying in his briefcase very full documentation of his expansionist plans, a killing that was one incident in the continuing private war the Russians and the Chinese have been waging against each other for a long time now. Alive, Long was a vital contributor to that burgeoning Chinese success story in terms of the world at large; dead, at least one chapter in this was brought to an abrupt ending. Moscow knew that he wouldn't be an easy man to replace. So did Peking. Long had been groomed carefully for his role of viceroy over the KKL empire, as well as bringing to it his own very real personal talents. But it was my bet that he had been a jealous viceroy, not allowing anything like a potential deputy anywhere near him. All that was left were characters like Mr Percy Smith whom, though I hadn't met him, I suspected would turn out to be deficient in the kind of dynamism that makes top men. It seemed pretty certain that the KKL organization would now not only fail to expand, but would soon start crumbling in on itself. In this connection I had to face the fact that without me Hok Lin Shipping, controlled by Nivalahannanda flair, might well go from strength to strength.

I had the use of my muscles again and sat very still wondering whether sudden action would serve me. There was no sign of the Colt Long had used on the floor which probably meant that it was in Johnny's pocket. Miss Wei was unarmed and wouldn't be able to stop my wild leap for freedom, but that grilled gate could and I didn't fancy being hunted in and out amongst illumined and dark shrubbery by a man with a silenced Luger. Also, I couldn't place the absentees from this room.

One of them came in, Johnny carrying the tape recorder. He swept broken glass off the drinks table to make room for it, then plugged the thing in. I listened to a hissing, then my own voice saying:

'It's a fine night.'

The hissing went on for all of five minutes and I was hoping Johnny would switch off, but he didn't and suddenly the late Long Kin said, in slightly bored tones:

'There are no signs of violence anywhere?'

Johnny turned up volume and I bellowed:

'Everything is perfectly tidy!'

'Extraordinary situation,' Long howled back.

Wei Linfen said something in Russian without looking up from her reading and the voices were mercifully softened to even below norm, but I didn't really enjoy that repeat performance. In the middle of it Jane arrived from the terrace carrying a bulky parcel of white plastic that must have been stowed in the convertible. She began to unroll this on the living-room floor, a body bag. I had a bad jolt when it seemed, for a moment, there were two of these.

There are not many parties of assassins who come prepared to be undertakers as well. It seemed probable that once he was parcelled K. K. Long would be thrown into the Macao current. He would have hated the idea. Chinese, even those who believe in nothing supranatural, which is most of them, want to be remembered by flashy, expensive funerals, a last flamboyant flourish with hired mourners screaming grief, a cymbal band, and huge paper models of the cars they would fancy for the world beyond if there was one. It is all ritual now, but not empty, meaningful for the neighbours who can price the show down to the last ten cent piece. I could see the performance for Long including forty foot scale models of his latest ships mounted on articulated lorries with firecrackers being shot off from the roofs of the driving cabs. Now, instead of leading a vast, noisy processional with pyrotechnics, he would go very quietly indeed in darkness, protected for a time from the little fishes by plastic, but not at all from sharks. If I travelled on the same death stream I wouldn't even rate the plastic.

I met a man once who told me he thought about dying every day of his life. Personally I don't like to, but what happened next in a Macao living-room didn't give me much chance to hit on another theme. Johnny brought in a large bath towel and Jane and he between them dragged the body by the ankles for its own length across flooring. Then, avoiding that slimy stream back from it, he lifted the corpse by the shoulders while Jane wrapped its head in a towel. After that they emptied the pockets, checking to see if Long carried anything to point to his identity. What was left of a man was then eased, towelling end first, into the bag, which was sealed by wide band adhesive tape. Jane straightened from functioning as a mortician's assistant to stand looking down at an outstretched arm. Blue silk was stained. Johnny said, in English :

'You should have rolled up your sleeves.'

She went out and there was the sound of water running from the bathroom. Johnny kept active without any instructions from Wei Linfen, as though he knew exactly what had to be done and was accustomed to doing it himself. Anything of Long's not travelling with him inside plastic was collected up for dropping into the briefcase, gold watch and lighter, wallet, small change, even an initialled handkerchief. The tape we had just listened to also went in. He brought the Luger over to his officer commanding and tucked this in against her right thigh, arranging it artistically so that the round mouth of the silencer piping seemed to be just on the point of having something to say to me. Miss Wei took custody of their main armament with a slight nod, but didn't look up from her reading, as absorbed as a suburban housewife who has finally got hold of the *Kama Sutra*. As Johnny straightened I saw the bulge of the Colt in a trouser pocket. He looked at me, really for the first time since that stare immediately after a kill, and what I saw in those eyes gave me the feeling that right now I was easily the worst life insurance risk in Macao and probably Hong Kong as well.

It was always a slight relief when he left the room. This time it was to switch out all the lights in the garden. The coloured fountain jets flickered, then expired. When the lamps in the living-room dimmed slightly I thought we were going to be plunged into total darkness, but they held on lowered strength which suggested a main fuse under stress from power suddenly needed for the radio transmitter. Five minutes later, a signal despatched, the bulbs brightened again.

Jane and Johnny reappeared, the girl with a wet sleeve. He said something in Russian which was important enough to make Wei Linfen look up. She continued to watch while the body was lifted, Johnny taking the heavy end, Jane the feet. The load looked a bit like too many dresses crammed into a moth-proof container, this with a sag in the middle. Reflections from glass shut away their progress across the terrace to the steps. Wei Linfen returned to her reading. If I had picked up the English version we might have looked a bit like a couple having a quiet home evening spurning television in favour of two library copies of the same thriller, but somehow I didn't feel I'd be able to get interested.

I stood up. Mongolian slits observed me and a hand

with longish fingernails rested on the Luger butt.

'Bathroom,' I said.

She was humane and allowed this, but I came back to find her slightly turned in her chair and waiting.

'Like a drink?' I asked.

'No.'

I poured for myself.

'Bring over the recorder when you come,' she said. 'You can plug it in here.'

'Isn't everything you need to know down in that agreement I haven't signed and wasn't going to?'

'I want a complete statement from you as well.'

'Then we'll have to have a new tape. I don't know where they're kept.'

'It will be in Ho Tai's room. Go and look.'

I went willingly enough but my bright idea came to nothing, the phone in the control-room had its lead ripped from the skirting. Johnny was trained to remember the little things. I could try locking the door and then putting out a May Day call on the radio or the walkie-talkie but it wouldn't be long before Wei Linfen blasted her way in to join me, perhaps having made a sudden decision to do without that complete statement. I found a new tape and took it back, standing to fit this, allowing myself a couple of sips of brandy but no more, it wasn't a time to become even slightly de-sensitized to what was happening around me.

I carried the box over, put it on the table next to the still open briefcase, found the plug and switched on.

'Where do you want me to begin?'

'Singapore. Your first contact with Long.'

'I had no contact with him in Singapore. I came up here to investigate OSL who seemed to be out to ruin my business. There was nothing then to point from them towards KKL.'

'Yet you went straight to Alvares?'

'On a tip I had in Hong Kong.'

'I see. Go on.'

But I didn't go on. From the garden came a scream of terror, wild, thin, a woman's.

CHAPTER XII

Wei Linfen was on her feet as quickly as I was, with the Luger in her hand. She was behind me as I ran out on to the terrace. A moving torch beam was briefly reflected by the black water in the pool, then the ray swung back on the paved surround. There were two people down there, and one of them was Jane Daly. She might have been running from a searchlight, expecting a stream of bullets to come after her along its alignment. Her evasive action, swinging out on grass, then back to paving again, didn't make much sense. She was like a rabbit leaping back and forth in front of car headlights, her pursuer gaining. If he had a gun he meant to use it at close range.

'It's Ho Tai! Give me that Luger!'

'No,' Miss Wei said.

'Damn you! Then get those bloody lights on! You're the servant. You know how to work them.'

On the steps I missed a tread, pitching into geraniums, sending a big pot crashing down on to paving beneath. The torch beam didn't sweep back towards the house, but I slithered the rest of the way, keeping low. The girl had stopped zig-zagging and was running all out for the deep end of the pool. She seemed to be almost holding the distance between her and that torch. Then she fell. The beam dropped. I saw the white of her face as she looked back. She rolled off into the water. Ho Tai set the torch down carefully so that its light shone out over the pool. He dived right on to the girl.

I ran past dressing-rooms and down the far side paving. Once I heard Jane shout, after that there was only splashing. I pulled off my jacket and dropped it. Japanese lanterns came on, together with the submerged blue bulbs. At the three-metre depth marker I kicked off shoes, filled my lungs and went in feet first, jack-knifing my body over to swim submerged, my eyes open. I saw their legs, the man's pumping as though he was riding a fixed exerciser, the girl doing a scissors kick that seemed to weaken as I swam towards them. I surfaced for air, then went down again, pushing myself to the bottom, toes touching it, looking up.

Jane wasn't kicking any longer. Ho Tai had her head under water, pushing her down against his body with his hands on her throat. I reached for one threshing ankle and caught it. My jerk down was cushioned by water but still sharp enough to make Ho Tai throw out his hands. He came down, Jane went up.

There hadn't been time for him to fill his lungs but he twisted towards me, open eyed. I flipped backwards but he caught one wrist. His other hand ripped down my shirt, then moved for my neck. His legs became tentacles around my hips. My free hand went for one of his eyes. His mouth opened, vomiting bubbles. We went up, surfacing still tangled, both gasping, his legs still a clamp. He pushed back, trying to ride my body as he gave himself room to start battering my head. I got in both fists just below his rib cage with enough force to break that clamp hold, then threw myself back from him. We both gulped in air. He hunched himself over to come at me again. I was spattered, not by water, something fractionally adhesive. Ho Tai had no face. I saw white bone before he sank. I turned my head. Wei Linfen was squatting on the pavement, the Luger held out in her right hand.

Jane Daly had her eyes shut when I got to her, though she was managing to hold on to the overflow ridge in the tiling. She had her mouth open as though to suck in air but her lung mechanism didn't seem to be working. Wei Linfen reached down with both hands and I pushed. We got her up on the paving. I had to swim slowly to steps to get out myself, then lay on my stomach to be sick. From back along the pool edging came a noise like a child caught in one of the uncontrollable spasms of whooping cough and there was also a slapping sound. I got up slowly, not looking at blue water. Wei Linfen carried on with her rough therapy while I found shoes and my jacket. Then I went back to where the girl was now sitting up, but with one leg splayed out as though dislocated. She had lost a sandal.

Between us we had almost to carry Jane, she couldn't get breathing back to anything like norm. When she had to be sick I was left to do the supporting, Wei Linfen just leaving us to go along past the dressing-rooms and then disappear behind the hibiscus hedge. Jane was bent over my arm. I put my free hand on her forehead. She pressed against it like a retching child in a nursery. I'd had my head held like this, too, years ago, by the Chinese amah who was my proxy mother.

We were walking again, Jane with much better control of her legs, when Wei Linfen reappeared, moving with that cat speed I had seen before, but this time Jane was the object of attack, words in Russian spat at her. It was a surprise when the girl who had been leaning on me suddenly shook off support and started to spit back. You can never really regiment women to the point where they will respect rank in all circumstances, even Russian women. I just stood there, not functioning as referee, but I did break it up, shouting in English:

'What the hell is all this?'

Miss Wei answered in Cantonese.

'She lost the key to the gate. When she was running. There's no time to look for it. You get up to the house and work that switch.'

'What's happened to Johnny?'

'Hit on the head. A car wrench.'

'Dead?'

'He's not dead.' That sounded almost bitter.

She had certainly lost calm, which happens to the best of us when suddenly faced with the need for a major planning reassessment. Arrangements had been made with great care to remove the remains of K. K. Long from the Villa Setubal, but now there was a second body in the pool and a man with probable concussion lying somewhere on a garden path. It was the kind of situation in which I prefer not to be officer commanding.

On the steps up to the terrace I tried to think of a swift and certain way to get rid of a briefcase, but needn't have bothered, it wasn't in the living-room, Wei Linfen had taken time to hide it some place down the path to the gate before she came along the edge of a pool to execute Ho Tai.

In Teng's room I took a clean shirt from a drawer. It was far too big, but dry. I dropped my own on the floor, put on my jacket, and went next door. The screen came alive to show the gate area still empty, and the mike didn't pick up any voices, though I heard the snarl of a car horn from somewhere down the hill. Immediately after that came another sound that sent a stinging to nerve endings, police sirens. These were swelling towards us. Neighbours probably hadn't heard the plop of a silenced Luger but someone had been disturbed by Jane's screaming and put in an alarm call.

Freedom of choice was handed back to me. This can be embarrassing at times. If I didn't join the escapees Wei Linfen couldn't now risk taking the time to come hunting for me with a gun. A good citizen would stay here to open the gate for the police. He would then tell the truth, the whole truth and nothing but the truth about how two bodies had come to have most of their heads shot away, going on to claim that he had been involved in all this only as the most innocent of bystanders. Even with Alvares as my lawyer an indefinite stay in a Portuguese jail seemed a certainty and cabled shouts for help to Superintendent Kang down in Singapore wouldn't do me much good. I was leaving.

Wei Linfen came on the screen. As I had suspected it would, a sudden emergency had dictated that a body in plastic be left for conventional disposal, and what she was dragging down the last steps to the gate area was Jane Daly. It was a fair-sized picture, the detail sharp, and I could even see the marks of a strangler's hands on the girl's neck. She seemed to have lost ground in her recovery from shock, weeping now, her jaw slack, her mouth open. Miss Wei slapped her hard on one cheek, then the other.

I opened the grille. Jane was used as the prop, pushed against metal flowers. She had lost the headscarf in the pool and wet blonde hair fell across her face as her head sagged forward. She looked very near to total collapse.

I switched off, then ran back through the glowing living-room. On the terrace the sirens sounded loud and near. I went down three steps at a time, throwing myself around the hibiscus hedge. At one of the S-bends on the path I nearly fell over a major obstacle.

This was a build up of bodies, Long's invisible in opaque plastic, Johnny's out at an angle from this. The golden boy's ice blue eyes were staring straight up at a night sky. His face was intact but the back of his head had been blown away by a Luger fired at close range to eliminate all traces of that earlier blow with a wrench. The long-snouted gun was there, too, at the end of Johnny's right arm bent back to suggest that he had himself fired the bullet which guaranteed that he would never talk to the Macao police. Wei Linfen had certainly not left loaded a gun I could pick up. I didn't touch anything. There were already too many of my fingerprints up in the house if local detectives turned up a clue pointing towards me.

She was waiting under the stone arch of the gate, with the Colt in her hand, the grille held back by one foot, and no sign of Jane. The noise of sirens was loud.

'You drive,' she said.

There were two cars to choose from, a Ford convertible pointing downhill and a Cadillac pointing up. It was no surprise to see the big car back in Macao, I hadn't thought the Chinese would allow it to travel any distance along their roads. Teng had been transhipped into something more suitable for use inside a socialist republic, Ho Tai ordered to take the offending monster back into the free world.

We were using the Cadillac. As Miss Wei held open a door for me I could just make out the shape of Jane in the back. I slid along a bench seat to behind the wheel, finding the ignition key at once but having trouble locating the lights' switch. I decided to start off without these, putting the gear into automatic drive, and stepping on the accelerator. I had a projectile under my hands, steering that take-off by one street lamp well up the road. When I finally got on our own lights these were bright enough to have brought in a jumbo jet, a white glare which picked colour out of stone walls and froze prowling cars.

'Turn right,' Wei Linfen said.

I forgot about the stern overhang on these cars and that sharp swing into a downhill lane brought us in contact with masonry, quite a crunch, after which we were accompanied by a percussion tune from torn steel.

'Left now.'

This time I got around without further damage and we came into a wider road lower down the hill, the suburb turning middle class, smaller villas half smothered in foliage. The descent was via tight bends and soft springing tossed us about. Jane behind was making no sound at all. She had a lot to think about, including the direct relevance to her own living of what had happened to Johnny. She was in a profession where an emergency could see a Comrade no longer a Comrade, just a risk factor to be eliminated. I wasn't anyone's Comrade, but recent happenings had a direct relevance to my future, too.

A glance at Miss Wei showed her hunched over. I got the feeling she wasn't pleased with herself. She was a tidy minded woman and meant to leave the Villa Setubal looking as neat as a summer place evacuated by a careful temporary tenant. Now it was strewn with corpses, but she had done her best in the circumstances, leaving one of these so arranged that it just might, with a stretch of imagination, serve to account for the other two. The police everywhere close some case dossiers which still have a lot of big question marks on the last page.

'Stop over there,' Wei Linfen ordered.

I was using my brakes when I realized that we were sliding in from the north towards the lane leading back to the Castello Blanco. At once Jane opened the back door and ran up towards our boarding-house, limping slightly on one bare foot, damp crinkled blue trousers up about her ankles.

'What's this for?'

'Be quiet,' Miss Wei said.

She was watching me and I didn't like it. Passers-by looked in at us but were more interested in the huge car, two boys standing in front of its massive façade to stare at this. I could just hear the engine bubbling away. A youth noticed our accident damage and pointed it out to a friend. Sitting behind that wheel I felt as though my own clock-work motor was being overwound to the point of its mainspring going. There would be a snapping noise when it did, followed by a thin metallic shriek from me, and after that someone else could drive.

Jane was coming back carrying my two suitcases and

my brown paper parcel. I was suddenly for this, hoping
she hadn't left anything, then had another thought which
was that after a few weeks, when I didn't show up any
place there would be no evidence to suggest that I had
disappeared from Macao. My landlady wouldn't complain, she had been paid.

Sirens were just audible again. They might have been the
reason why Jane dropped one of the suitcases, humping all
that stuff hard for the kind of girl who could always get
a porter anywhere. But for all this hold-up there was no
pursuit from Mama defending a lodger's property. Jane
got one case and the parcel into the back of the car, then
returned for the other. I saw her face as she climbed in
herself, this blank, eyes staring.

I had to drive carefully, edging the Cadillac past other
traffic, not sure that some of the gaps offered were wide
enough. The spacious Praya was a release. Not much
of the wheeled traffic seemed to be going our way and I
got up to seventy. We passed the casino ship, then the
Algarve Hotel, glowing with profits. I heard sirens again,
not one but an intermezzo for thinned woodwinds beamed
down on us by the city's acoustics. The air-conditioner
was on but there were drops of sweat on my forehead.

'When we get to the park don't go around the corner,'
Wei Linfen said.

'You mean we stop there?'

'No. You drive up on the pavement by the sea wall.'

'Don't be crazy! There isn't room for this thing.'

'There is enough.'

'But there could be people in there?'

'No matter! You will get this car into shadow!'

We were out of the area used by strollers, the pavements
empty. I braked, bumping up over a kerb into the gap between a massive retaining wall and a projecting rock
garden, putting wheel emphasis on the rockery side which
looked less likely to be resistant. Some ornamental stone-

work tried to stop us but I accelerated through, bringing down a small avalanche of earth behind the car.

There was no getting past the statue of a former governor, he was dead stop. But we were in shadow. Suddenly from bushes, and as though fear had kept them quiet during a tank attack, a man and a girl got up to come blundering past, running for the Praya lights. A siren came down the avenue but went screaming around the corner.

Miss Wei opened her door. Mine was against the sea wall. I slid over.

'You carry your bags,' she said, handing me one, then the other, waiting until my hands were full before attending to Jane, who now seemed to be in hiding.

Something was tossed over the sea wall wrapped in a yellow duster. It could have been a car wrench bearing traces of hair and congealed blood. Our processional, to a tune of sirens, was Jane first carrying my parcel and K. K. Long's briefcase, now bulging, me with my bags, then Wei Linfen with a Colt in one hand and flashlight in the other.

I knew where we were going. Ho Tai had brought me this way, to the ending of the esplanade and down a flight of steps leading to a rocky path. About a quarter of a mile along this was a cobbled beach used for drying fishing nets. There were no houses and no lights, a safe enough rendezvous if there was no pursuit, but we had left behind us a clear pointer as to where we had gone and if there wasn't a boat waiting for us on that beach we would all be eating Portuguese police-station breakfasts in the morning. If there was a boat I would be travelling on it, Wei Linfen hadn't got her statement yet, which meant that her documentation was still incomplete.

A siren cut out suddenly and though the big rocks around us might be deflecting sound, I was pretty sure a police car was now emptying out its passengers near a damaged rock garden. Jane gave a little cry and stumbled, nearly falling. Miss Wei flicked on her torch and lifted the beam.

Dead ahead of us were two figures standing close in to a boulder as though ready to use it for cover. They were in black wetsuits, the frogmen outfits complete except for flippers and face masks. One of them had an automatic rifle and had selected me for target.

Wei Linfen called out in Russian. The gun was lowered.

I found a submarine's crash dive almost as nerve tightening as those moments of getting airborne when you wonder whether engines are going to be able to develop maximum thrust. In both cases you are pushing into an element where man is an intruder, the one meant for birds, the other for fish. Certainly there is much less noise going down but almost at once you are conscious of water pressure, or I was. I sat remembering old movies showing all the things that can happen to keep one of these steel cylinders from ever surfacing again, like a leak through the torpedo tube doors.

I was in the smallest cabin I had ever seen, just room for a berth and my feet on the deck, not even a washbasin with a tap. A ravenous hunger had been only half assuaged by a cup of the kind of cocoa the Soviets get on barter deals with emergent nations, plus a large hard biscuit apparently issued to crew to keep their teeth sharp. I shared the bunk with my two suitcases and a *sang-de-boeuf* vase I hadn't much hope of being able to deliver to Amelia. My clothes, taken away wet after about a dozen miles at speed in an inflatable rubber dinghy, had been returned dry but stiff and I had put them on again to find that every time I moved I creaked. My shock-proof, water-proof, heavily guaranteed watch had given me up and stopped. I had a headache which said that if I lay down it would get worse so I just sat. The light was harsh

and there was no way to put it out. All this left me ready
for nothing when the door opened.

Jane Daly was in a semi-uniform of grey trousers and
tunic, but without insignia of rank. Her beautiful hair was
now drawn back from her face to a bun low on the neck
but she still didn't look like a school-teacher, or even what
she was, an undercover agent who hadn't stood up too well
to a stress test. There had been moments during our last
hour or two in Macao when I had almost felt a warmth
towards this girl, and a faint hangover from this still
survived even when she took out a notebook and pencil.

She did this out in the passage, the cabin didn't offer
much space for arm movements, and, ready for the inter-
view, she then contrived to get in with me and shut the
door, leaning back on it. I could have offered her space on
the bunk but I had a feeling the invitation would be refused, as creating too informal an atmosphere. This was an
interrogation. Only Wei Linfen could have sent in a
junior colleague, still not totally recovered from shock, to
do a job like this while she herself sat listening to the
recording in an adjoining cell, probably with her feet up.
My impulse to make it easier for Jane was almost certainly
silly, but it showed humane feelings surviving even when
I couldn't personally expect to be on the receiving end of
these. There was also the fact that if we didn't seem to
be coming across too well on tape Wei Linfen might take
over herself, and I didn't want that. So I co-operated.
For one thing it bought time and if they had enough of this
my captors might come up with some ideas, other than
the obvious one, about what to do with me later.

'Your full name?' Jane was looking at a bulkhead as
though she didn't need to watch what she wrote down.

We went right through my childhood, adolescence and
youth and by the time we were ready for maturity I was
terribly thirsty. Jane's voice kept trying for a cold, probing
neutrality but never quite achieved this and it was only

when we got to my role as an exploiter of the toiling masses that she seemed to become in any way personally involved in this session, as though her honours subject at college was suddenly fed in, to give her some real support. Her notes became more careful during this phase and she even looked at me, glances that were an imitation of an earlier savage contempt. But the zeal had gone out of her. If I'd been in a position to offer advice I'd have suggested that if she was allowed to go to Mauritius after this that she resign her commission immediately on arrival, grab the first half-French planter she met and settle at once to adding to the over-population problem on an island already bursting at the seams.

After about an hour I gave up trying to defend myself against charges of neo-colonialism, my answers going on automatic like her questions. Sometimes I looked at her and sometimes at the deck, and during brief silences, which she jumped in to eliminate, I heard the rumble of engines and felt vibration. At one point I had a sudden urge to wreck the tape by asking whether she, too, in Macao had walked the streets with her love, knowing now that Johnny Cass had been much more than another body on a bed, knowing this with hideous clarity during those moments when a bitch from hell had put a bullet in his skull.

There was a ten-minute break when I said I couldn't go on without a drink of water, Jane leaving the cabin to get this. I sat thinking about Wei Linfen. Possibly this was telepathic and the lady from a yak skin tent was beamed right in on me, too, in which case I hope she got the only compliment I had to send her, full marks for courage. It could be that she was now travelling in this submarine to Vladivostok, scheduled to fly on from there to a well-earned holiday in the Crimea, but in view of that untidy ending to her recent mission it was more likely to be straight back to duty. I could see a night-landing on the China coast somewhere, Wei Linfen once again alone, another of Moscow's secret strangers within the vast expanse of an enemy's territory, self-contained, dedicated, trained in making all the Mao-orientated noises. There can be no lonelier life, the motivation for it to me inconceivable, and I could only wonder if she had her moments of weakness in the breath-laden darkness of some commune or factory dormitory, lying to remember the desert of her youth, the great sweep of the Steppes, the free running horses, and the unchained patterns of her nomad, roaming people. An ugly woman, painted as a whore and practising the craft when this was necessary, accepting assignments involving murder, but living in her mind for a cause, really an ascetic.

Jane came back with the water, after which we went on again for what felt like nearly two hours through which she stood the whole time, part of her penance. At the end of it was my throat was raw and my mind ached. I couldn't feel, either, that my life stood up well to a hundred thousand spoken words, all that tape they had piled up somewhere simply crying out for a *Reader's Digest* condensation. Jane looked in worse shape than I felt, her face drawn. She put away the notebook and pencil in a tunic pocket and was going through the complicated manœuvre of opening the door when I put a last word on to plastic.

'Goodbye.'

She stared at me. I thought for a moment she was going to say something, but she didn't.

I was sitting at a control panel very like the one at the Villa Setubal. There was a picture on the screen in front of me, a bare-walled room with a table and four chairs. Three of the chairs were occupied. Facing was K. K. Long, most of his body screened by a briefcase, just his head visible over the top of it. On his right was Johnny Cass and on his left Ho Tai. They were arguing about something, Johnny vehement, thumping a fist on the table, though I couldn't hear the noise from that or a word of what was being said. I twisted dials trying desperately to get sound for the picture, but none came. I was certain their subject was me and as though to confirm this Ho Tai suddenly turned in his chair and his face, mouth opened for a shout, swelled to fill the screen as if it wasn't that, but a glass panel, and he could see me on the other side.

I woke sweating. Wei Linfen was standing close in, to the bunk looking down at me. I drew the back of my hand across eyes and a damp forehead but when I let it drop again she was still there.

'You've had a good rest, Harris?'

I pushed myself up against a bulkhead. One of my legs, which had been twisted about a suitcase, came awake more slowly than the rest of me, full of pins and needles.

'If you discount a couple of nightmares, yes.'

She was very near, but that didn't tell me much. When your face is made up of minimal features, eye cracks, and a thin layer of skin drawn as tightly over protuberant cheekbones as an actress's after the second face lift, there isn't much play left in it for expression. Talking to Miss Wei when she wasn't wearing make-up didn't give the feeling of being in contact with a personality at all. She could paint one on, achieving interesting effects, but after the soap and water treatment was just a prototype, suggesting a mock-up still in the most rudimentary stages of design.

Janey, in her near uniform without rank tabs, had contrived to look a bit like a worker in a Russian ladies' auxiliary corps, but there was no hint of this with Wei Linfen who continued to wear blue denims as though she had just come in from a hard day's work in the paddy fields. This rather confirmed my feeling that she wasn't staying on the submarine for long.

My throat was still slightly dry but the headache had gone which was something. I waited, certain that I was in for a supplementary questioning on points which had arisen during a detailed consideration of my statement on tape. This forecast was correct.

'You phoned a waiter in a café from the Villa Setubal?'

'Yes.'

'He knew where you were when you rang?'

I nodded.

'Would he recognize you from a photograph?'

'I should think so. His kind don't often come in contact with big tippers. But the Macao police would have a job getting hold of a picture of me. I never have them taken. On picnics I'm the one who holds the camera.'

'A wise precaution.'

'I believe so. I can see what's worrying you, Miss Wei, but I don't think I'd let it too much.'

'What do you mean by that?'

'Just suggesting that there will be very little, if any, publicity about what the police discovered at the Villa Setubal. Officially it will be accepted that Johnny shot himself when it was clear he was going to be trapped in the garden with the two men he had killed.'

'Why?'

'Because the order to do that will come from north of the border. Macao obeys those orders. Neither Long nor Johnny will ever be properly identified. Long was travelling as Mr Pu. No one knows about Mr Pu except a few of his staff. I don't think you had uncovered that identity, either?'

She said nothing. I could just see her eyes behind those slits and in that moment I was perfectly certain that the matter of my future had been referred to HQ by radio signal, Miss Wei receiving the reply that she was to do what she thought best in the circumstances. I was completely in her hands. If ever a man had a strong incentive to take a convincing initiative I did.

'Why should China issue such an order, Harris?'

'Because what you managed to do in Macao represents

a serious defeat for them. One of the advantages of a half-secret war is that in most cases you don't have to admit a defeat. KKL shipping will continue for some time as before, even though mortally crippled. Its death, if that happens, will be a slow one. And with a lot of hard work going on in the resuscitation unit to keep the patient alive.'

'Which you don't think will be successful?'

'No, I don't. Nor do you. Otherwise you wouldn't have been out just to eliminate Long. But now all those other companies at present operating in the Indian Ocean are quite safe from KKL competition. At least for a number of years.'

'And your Hok Lin is also safe?'

'I hope so.'

'You are quite pleased that Long Kin is eliminated?'

'Surely you don't expect me to regret the death of a man who would have shot me if you hadn't killed him? Also, as I told Johnny Cass, I'm not against the Soviet presence out here. I think we need such a presence to be a buffer against China, and you're the only serious candidate for the role that I can see. As a man whose interests are in these parts it is greatly to my advantage to have two giants at each other's throats. It gives us little people a chance to survive more or less unnoticed.'

She leaned back against a bulkhead, the first time I had seen her do anything to suggest that she might, on occasion, feel tired. Suddenly she said :

'You are an imperialist pirate !'

'Cut out the imperialist and I might accept that.'

There was no hint of a smile.

'The liquidation of men like you is part of our purpose.'

'I know. But let's make it a long-term purpose, shall we? And meantime I'm just a small operator, as I made plain to K. K. Long. I want to stay that way. I do no harm to anyone at all.'

'That's not my opinion!' A moment later she said: 'If you are landed in Hong Kong what will you do?'

'Fly home as soon as possible.'

'Without your passport?'

'An assistant ought now to have arrived from Singapore with the necessary replacement.'

'Why wasn't this in your statement?'

'I was answering questions. My future didn't come into them.'

Wei Linfen reached out to open the door. She edged along and stepped backwards through it, standing in the passage for a moment to look in at me. It seemed a long moment. She put out a hand and pulled the door shut, leaving me frightened.

I was still frightened when a sailor came in bringing another mug of cocoa and this time a ham sandwich. He looked a bit like Johnny Cass, tall and fair with blue eyes, but an innocent, not bright enough for a really important career, lucky fellow. He watched me eat, then produced a roll of wide band Elastoplast, indicating that this was for my eyes. I grabbed at the thought that there isn't much point in blindfolding a man you plan to push off the whaleback of a submarine into the South China Sea. This was the first cheer I'd had for some time and I hung on to it, docile while he fitted the stuff well up over my eyebrows and patted it down into the cavities by my nose.

Travel under a personal blackout has its own interest, sharpening up the other senses. I was led through an area where all sound pinged off steel, up a ladder and out into air which felt roughly fresh. After that it was some time in a rubber boat powered by an outboard. The engine cut and we drifted, a word or two spoken, a throat cleared, the smell of tobacco and the sound of very small waves lapping. Then a heavy diesel beat came towards us and I was pushed up a rope ladder for about the right distance to land me on the well deck of a junk. I sat again, this time near a guard with a smoker's cough.

The feeling behind this journeying was remarkably relaxed, no sense of tension at any stage, and certainly Hong Kong has the highest incidence of illegal landings in the world, so what happened to me was probably routine. In the final phase I lay on the floorboards of a small sampan listening to the creaking of a stern oar and the screeching of gulls. After a time I slept, woken by a gentle bump and whispering in Cantonese.

This time the climb up wasn't much more than a stretch, over a low railing. I was guided to a seat and heard my luggage being put down around about, but no sound of feet going away, the only human noise coming across water, a couple of women shouting. There was the hoot of a car horn.

The best way to take off Elastoplast is the doctor's technique, work up a corner and then rip. I did this without screaming, looking down to see that most of my eyebrows had stayed with the adhesive. After the last few days the loss of some facial hair seemed unimportant.

I was sitting on a bench at the stern of the lower cooking deck of one of the floating restaurants permanently anchored off Taplishan, which is also known as Aberdeen, and facing the semi-permanent community of junks not more than a couple of hundred yards away. Between me and the boats one of the sampan taxis rowed by old women was already in operation. I shouted and she heard at once, turning her craft. No one came out of the restaurant's still silent kitchens.

Amelia Jackson's apartment block was only half-way up the Peak, middle-income bracketing, but it still had a wonderful view, the bay, Kowloon, the New Territories green in morning light, and then the distant hills of real China. I went up in the lift, along a corridor, pressed a bell and waited. Wisely she opened the door on a chain.

'Who's that?'

Her hair was in curlers.

'Paul Harris.'

'What? Oh, my goodness me! However did you . . .?'

'I'm not coming in. I want to deliver this. I've got a taxi waiting.'

'Don't be crazy. You *are* coming in. Go right down and pay off your driver. I was just going to make breakfast and you'll have it with me. And bring up your bags. You can't leave anything lying around these days.'

By the time I was up again with the bags she was in a cotton housecoat, had her hair combed out, and tied back with a ribbon and there was a smell of coffee. It was quick work.

'Paul, how did you get here? There's no night ferry.'

'Private hire.'

'Well . . .? What's in that package you gave me?'

'A replacement vase.'

We had it with us in the breakfast bar, and the light was good, but somehow I couldn't see the depth of colour in the glaze it had appeared to have in Macao. It was still a pretty vase and Amelia put on a great act of liking it and what a fortune it must have cost, but Boonville wasn't going to be the home of a really good imitation King-teh-chen. After breakfast I rang the Mandarin Hotel from the living-room.

'Has a Mr Bahadur from Kuala Lumpur checked in?'

'Just a moment, please.'

The moment was long enough for Amelia to come in with the vase and try it in various places, standing back from a piece of art like a member of the selection committee for an exhibition. Wherever she put it the thing still looked what it was.

'Hallo, caller? We have no Mr Bahadur registered. But there is a *Mrs* Bahadur.'

'That's ridiculous,' I said. 'But it'll have to do.'

The Mandarin sets out to remind its guests that they are in China, or at least in nice, pretty safe, British China. There are all kinds of little features that do this. I went over to the desk and tested to see how Mrs Bahadur reacted to Paul Harris. I was told to go right up, the suite was on the seventh floor. If that boy thought I was paying for suites he was in for a shock.

'Yes. Come in.'

I knew the voice. I opened the door with caution. Ranya Nivalahannanda was stretched out on a sofa looking like a Siamese Récamier, the same flowing lines of negligee which said the wearer was a woman who thought about men and nothing but men. After a submarine she looked beautiful.

'Hallo, Paul.'

'What's this Mrs Bahadur stuff?'

'I thought the name might be significant and that you wouldn't come out of hiding unless you heard it. You look tired. And what's the matter with your face? Your eyebrows . . .?'

'I'm wearing them thinner this season. Where's my man from Kuala Lumpur?'

'Still there. It seemed better that I come. I've brought what you need to get home. Batim Salong did everything at speed. He's sweet, for a prince.'

'How did you find Bahadur?'

'He's sweet, too.'

'Nonsense! He hates women.'

'Not me,' Ranya said. 'He's coming to work for us in Singapore.'

'Like hell he is!'

'As my personal assistant. My secretary has left. She didn't like being on probation. I told her she was lucky we're not prosecuting. I thought you'd want to be generous? So I'll just use the typing pool and have a beautiful

Sikh by me all the time. Paul, have you been having it rough?'

'Yes.'

'Well, sit down and tell me about it.'

'Later. There's too much for now.'

'Have you had breakfast?'

I nodded.

'Who with?'

'An American. We had waffles and maple syrup.'

'You mean *that* woman? You travelled from Macao together?'

'No. It seemed more discreet to come separately. When did you get here?'

'Last night. I had a wonderful evening with Ralph.'

'Ralph who?'

'Ralph P. Brinkhausen.'

I stared at her.

'You mean that man is in the Mandarin?'

'Yes. One floor down. It seemed more discreet. Paul, *do* sit down.'

'What does he want with me?'

'I think he'd better tell you that himself.'

'Which means you still don't know?'

'Oh, I know all right. Five minutes after we met the security curtain was lifted. And on the plane from Singapore we found out what a lot we have in common. Last June he divorced the third Mrs Brinkhausen. It seems to take a lot of money to lose a wife in Texas. He had to pay her one and a half million dollars down and fifty thousand dollars a year for life. Isn't that *awful*?'

Ranya could really feel for anyone who paid alimony, having had to do it herself for years.

'You found out how much Brinkhausen has got left?' I asked.

She smiled.

'Somewhere between thirty-three and thirty-four million dollars depending on the state of the stock market.'

It looked like he could afford a couple more divorces, even with inflation. The thought had certainly occurred to Ranya. She was looking serene as she always did when mentally active.

'You want me to ring his suite, Paul?'

'Not yet. Why is he chasing me?'

'To make an offer for your Scotch shipyard.'

'*What*?'

She waited to let the full implications of the news sink in, then said:

'His company has a big slice of North Sea oil. They need specialist ships to service the rigs and your yard is the right size for adapting to do this. He's been over there to have a look at it.'

There had practically been pilgrimages to look at my yard.

'Why are you staring at me like that?' Ranya asked. 'I thought you'd be wild with joy. That place has been around your neck for years.'

'I was thinking I might build those specialist ships myself. '

I got her sweet smile again.

'Ralph says that he figures automating and modernizing will cost at least three million dollars initially and probably five million before he starts getting a return on his money. You have that kind of capital available?'

She knew down to a few hundred or so how much capital I had available without selling my gold watch which still wasn't working.

'I want to consider this,' I said.

'Of course. Why not take five minutes now to do that?'

'I'll do it in a bath. I've shaved but I didn't like to ask Amelia if I could use her tub. Mind if I use yours?'

'Help yourself.' There was a pause, then she added:

'Amelia is a horrible name.'

'It's not the name that matters, it's the warm loving heart.'

I went through the bedroom to the kind of plumbing that would have appealed to a Roman emperor, but when I was deep in hot water I didn't think about a Scots shipyard at all, just Wei Linfen. It was almost as though she had come through to me loud and clear and a telepathic line from a submarine submerged somewhere off Swatow. I hadn't been pushed into the South China Sea thirty miles from the nearest landfall simply because my potential usefulness, under pressures to be evolved later, outweighed the security risk of letting me go. It was one of the nastiest signals ever to reach me. Even when I added more hot water with my toes I still felt cold.

The door opened. Ranya said:

'Want your Thai woman to scrub your back?'

She wasn't exactly the kind of girl against whose comforting breasts you could rest your weary head, but she was the nearest thing I had to it.

'Yes,' I said.